Lord Crispin O'Neill, returning to Liverpool from Jamaica in the middle of the eighteenth century, feels confident that his offer of marriage will be accepted by the beautiful Miss Pamela Courtney. Then, on the point of return from the West Indies, Crispin realises he does not have a homecoming present for his intended bride. By the dockside, a pretty slave-girl is being auctioned and impulsively his lordship buys Peri—the perfect gift for Pamela.

Alas, Pamela and her unusual 'gift' dislike each other on sight. Complications multiply when Crispin's rakish cousin attempts to seduce Peri, so how can his lordship possibly hope to defend the innocent little French girl without losing all hope of marrying the rich and spirited Miss Courtney?

A Gift for Pamela

Judy Turner

MILLS & BOON LIMITED
London · Sydney · Toronto

*First published in Great Britain 1981
by Mills & Boon Limited, 15–16 Brook's Mews,
London W1A 1DR*

© Judy Turner 1981

*Australian copyright 1981
Philippine copyright 1981*

ISBN 0 263 73441 2

Set in VIP Baskerville 11 on 12½ pt
by Fakenham Press Limited

*Made and printed in Great Britain by
Cox & Wyman Ltd., Reading*

For Rosemarie and Doug Hague,
cousins, friends and wonderful people.

CHAPTER
ONE

THE *Snow Tempest* edged her way through the narrow channel which led from the Mersey estuary into the Old Dock, following the tugs like a great swan in pursuit of cygnets. Crispin, Lord O'Neill, standing on the deck watching the manoeuvre, felt the cold wind on his face and was glad he had dressed as a gentleman should, in the embroidered coat and breeches, the silk stockings, the square-toed shoes which he had been happy to manage without during the voyage. Then, he had worn a shirt and a pair of sailor's breeks, but with their return to colder waters he had been glad enough to conform to fashion once more.

He glanced down at his hands on the rail, seeing the even tanning of his skin and thinking how his favourite sister, Selina, would tease him, for it would be no excuse during the Season that he had but lately returned from his estates in Jamaica. Labourers might be brown; gentlemen, never!

He glanced at his small bag, set down beside him on the deck with his surtout on top of it. It held his personal things, so must be carried off the ship with him now. The luggage in the hold was a different matter. He must arrange for it to be delivered to Brownlow Hall as soon as possible, for it contained all his presents, including his wedding present for Selina; a fabulous pearl necklace whose cost still caused him to wince a little.

The *Snow Tempest* was turning now, the men on shore coaxing her into the place which awaited her. Sails had been lowered out in the estuary and now the sailors made fast and the gangplank was lowered.

Lord O'Neill picked up his surtout and struggled into it, shaking out the silk of his stock, adjusting the diamond pin which held it in place, glad that recent fashion had caused many young men to forsake wigs in favour of their own hair. He clapped his laced hat on over his curls, however, and strolled towards the gangplank.

He was not expected; indeed, had it not been for the change of plans which had brought Selina's marriage forward, he would not have been in England now, for his original intention had been to remain in Jamaica for a further month. However, when the news had reached him of the change of date he had booked a passage on the *Snow Tempest* immediately and thanks to favourable winds he would surprise his family with an arrival quite a week earlier than they would have supposed possible.

As he reached the cobbled quay, the sun came out for a moment, lighting up the busy scene. There was a good crowd milling about before the Custom House and his lordship supposed, vaguely, that they were waiting for an auction to commence. A couple of pretty, painted young women passed, eyeing him boldly, and one of them made Lord

O'Neill halt in his tracks. She was a yellow-head, rouged and grimy, yet she reminded him sharply of someone.

Whilst he hesitated, the elusive resemblance burst on him like a thunderclap. Pamela! He groaned, clutching his head. How could he have forgotten her? The most sought-after belle during her first season, and she had shown a decided preference for him. She was to be one of his sister's bridal attendants, would be ensconced in the house at this very moment, and he had not brought her a gift!

Standing still and allowing the crowd to mill around him, Lord O'Neill closed his eyes and feverishly tried to recall the contents of those boxes still down in the *Tempest*'s·hold. Silks? Pamela had more clothes than any other female of his acquaintance. What about the beautiful, hand-painted china, so translucent that when held up to the light, one could see one's fingers curled round the cup? But it had been intended for the Dowager Lady O'Neill; he could not deprive her of a gift which she would love so much.

He thought of the other things, so carefully chosen. Native carvings on hard wood, on ivory, on hand-cured leather. Huge, brilliantly coloured sea-shells. Branches of coral and soft, exciting sea-sponges.

He sighed, opening his eyes. It was no use. He would have to rush round to Dale Street, which was the best shopping district in Liverpool, and see if he could find something suitable. He remembered her pale beauty, the way her big blue eyes smiled on him, and swallowed. Fancy forgetting Miss Pamela Courtney! Well, she must never suspect such a thing. He would find something to show her that he had thought of her constantly in his absence; something unusual.

He moved to make his way off the dock, and as he turned his head, a commotion broke out on board the *Snow Tempest*. He glanced up at the deck. Were they beginning to unload the cargo already? He saw a sailor emerge from the hold with someone, smaller than himself, close beside him. Other sailors emerged and a closer look solved the mystery.

Slaves! He had not realised that whilst he, travelling as supercargo, enjoyed the best that the ship could provide, slaves had been confined in the hold. His straining eyes saw that they were all females, half-a-dozen of them, each woman roped round one wrist and held by a sailor, each naked save for a brief sarong of brilliant cotton stuff.

They descended the gangplank and filed past him, making for the Custom House. Now that they were close he saw that they were all handsome, for the most part a little above average height, their skin tones varying from blue-black to coffee, and they looked more intelligent than the terrified Negroes he had watched as they were driven off the slave ships in the harbour at St Kitts and auctioned off to the callous and indifferent planters.

And then the last slave came down the gangplank. She was some way behind the others for some reason, and the sailor holding her wrist-rope was tugging her along, trying to catch up. Lord O'Neill's eyes flickered over her orange sarong, the delicious creamy gold of her skin, and then fixed themselves on her face. A small, heart-shaped face with a straight little nose, a kissable mouth and a pair of large, dark eyes. As she passed him their glances met and locked and she smiled at him, a defiant little smile, making her look more vulnerable, somehow, than she had seemed before. Then she was past, and he could see only the waves of dark hair which fell to her knees like a cloak as she was tugged and cuffed up the Custom House steps.

Lord O'Neill followed until he reached the foot of the steps. He told himself that since he had not seen an auction of slaves before, he might as well stay for a moment. But his gaze was fixed on the small creature in the orange sarong standing at the top of the steps, wide eyes fixed on the people beneath her.

The auctioneer, with a businesslike air, pulled the girl forward by one wrist. He was turning her round, extolling her points as though she had been a horse, and Lord O'Neill, normally a mild young man, felt his hackles rise.

'*And* pretty,' the auctioneer was saying, with a world of meaning in his tone. 'She'd be a pleasant addition to any household or business. Let's hear some bids now, gentlemen!'

Near to him, a thickset man whom his lordship recognised as a prosperous mill-owner said thickly, 'A pleasant addition indeed! I'd find a use for her.' He chuckled, and named an amount.

Quickly, another voice called out. The child—for she was little more—on the steps was staring from face to face, her hands clasping and unclasping, her tongue coming out to wet fright-dry lips.

The bids were coming thick and fast. The mill-owner glared at his chief opponent, a hard-faced woman in her mid-fifties who ran a large bawdy-house down by the docks. Suddenly, the bawdy-house owner leaned towards the thickset man. 'If I buy the wench, you shall have her first!' she declared.

For a moment, his lordship quite literally saw red. With a growl of fury he seized the two bidders by their shoulders and flung them aside so that he could mount the steps two at a time to push his face, his eyes smouldering furiously, close to the auctioneer's startled countenance.

'She's *sold*, damn you,' he heard his own voice saying curtly. 'Sold!' He fished in his pocket, bringing out a roll of bills, hearing his own voice once again naming a preposterous sum.

In a daze, he caught her wrist and looked down into the big, dark-lashed eyes. The auctioneer was bringing the next woman forward, and as he passed back down the steps and through the curious crowd, someone said enviously, 'Cor! Does he own a tavern, or a play'ouse? Why did he buy her? That was a mint o' money!'

And unbidden, Lord O'Neill heard his voice saying pleasantly, 'She's a gift for Pamela. That's it, the very thing! A gift for Pamela!'

.   .   .   .

The girl looked up at the tall, handsome young man whose eyes had kindled with appreciation when he had looked on her as she passed him in the crowd, and felt the first beginnings of happiness stir within her. He had bought her, this fair-haired Englishman with brilliant blue eyes and skin tanned a clear nut-brown! After the voyage from Africa to Jamaica she was without illusions; he would doubtless take her as his mistress. Men either wanted a mistress or a worker, and she knew herself to be small and slight compared with the other slaves on the Custom House steps.

As he led her through the crowd she glanced up at him, seeing the determined jawline, the set of his firm lips. His mistress! A delicious shiver of apprehension coursed through her. On the ship she had dreaded that she would be forced by some filthy, degraded seaman. She had seen many fellow-slaves suffer that fate.

In fact, her own poor condition had saved her. When she had been taken aboard the *Tempest* she had been weak, exhausted from her long trek in the slave train, and filthy. On board ship her skin had come out in great, ugly blotches of eczema, due to the inadequate diet and to the daily hosings in sea-water which had worsened her condition.

During the voyage to England, however, she had been well-treated, for the captain knew that only slaves in excellent condition would make good prices from the canny Liverpudlians. And by the time they reached the harbour, she was glowing with health and high spirits once more.

Now, trotting to keep up with the long strides of her rescuer, she could not keep the hero-worship from shining in her eyes whenever she looked at him. He had saved her from the fat, disgusting old man whose eyes had stripped from her even the slight protection of her cotton sarong, and from the cruel, hard-eyed woman who had shouted out her bids so loudly.

He was leading her away from the quayside and the docks. They were traversing a broad street which widened ahead of them into a pleasant square, when he drew her to a halt and looked consideringly down at her.

'My God, I can't walk into Brownlow Hall with you dressed like that! Do you speak English? What's your name?'

'I speak English, yes. My name is Rachelle Blanche Nicolette Perigand.'

He blinked, his brows flying up almost to his hairline.

'Rachelle Blanche what? Are you French? Then whatever are you doing being sold as a slave in Liverpool?' He frowned down at her, anxious to understand. 'Yes, damme, you've got a French accent!'

'My Papa was French,' she said slowly. The English she had scarcely spoken for years had not been easy to recapture at first, but after months spent aboard a ship where the only common language had been English, the old knack had returned. 'My Mama was English, and it was our secon' language, at home. It is a long story.'

He grinned down at her. 'So I'll warrant! It seems wrong that you are my slave, yet I bought you fair and square.'

She caught hold of his hand, pressing it fervently between her own small palms. 'Oh, yes, m'sieur, I am your slave! My parents, they died many years ago, when I was a little child. They had a plantation off the coast of Africa and after the deaths, two of the Negro slaves stole a boat and rowed back to the mainland. They took me wiz ... with them as a hostage, and reared me for many seasons. But there was a man ...' She grimaced, still holding his hand tightly within her own. 'A trader he was, a Portuguese. He wanted to marry me but I did not want to marry him! So I ran away, and fell in wiz bad people, who sold me to the slave traders. I *tole* them I was half English, half French, but they said too bad! I was a slave unless relatives came with money and bought me!'

'I see. And you've no relatives living, that you know of?'

'No. But I have you, now. You'll look after me, yes?'

Lord O'Neill swallowed. 'Well, in fact I bought you for ... but you'll be taken care of, I promise you that.' He began to walk again, leading her to one side of the square where horses and carriages stood. 'The trouble is, I'd not thought, but it might look strange ...' He stopped beside one of the carriages, shouting to the jarvey on the box that he wanted to be taken to the lodge at Brownlow Hall. Glancing down at his charge, he went on, 'Into the carriage with you, child, and we'll talk this out. I'll ... I'll make suitable arrangements for you once I'm home.'

She hung back, eyeing the dark interior of the carriage with trepidation. 'In there? You want that I go in there? And you will come too? You won't leave me?'

He found her trust in him touching if a trifle misplaced, considering that she was bought as a present for someone else, and as such, would not be with him for very long. But he nodded, and then, when she still hung back, lifted her up in his arms and dumped her bodily down upon the cracked leather upholstery, then sank into the seat opposite.

'I was going to get in,' she announced, patting the seat curiously, 'but I was a little afraid, perhaps.' She smiled at him, showing a row of perfect little white teeth. 'Oh, but I am heavy for you! I make you to breathe hard!'

Lord O'Neill, who had been unprepared for the sensation of holding an almost naked girl in his arms, cleared his throat and changed the subject.

'You mustn't be afraid when I leave you presently. It will only be for a short while. You see, my family aren't expecting me, and most certainly they won't expect me to bring a ... a slave home with me! You must be suitably dressed before I can take you up to the Hall. But I've had an idea. Do you know what a nurse is?'

'Yes, of course! I had a nurse till Mama and Papa died. She was a Negress, though, Mammy Lucia. She took me to her own tribe after the fever had killed my parents.'

'I see. Well, my nurse isn't a Negress, but she's a very old lady, and lives in retirement at the lodge near my home. She'll look after you, and find you suitable clothing, and teach you how to behave.'

The small face opposite his own scowled abruptly. 'I know how to behave! I am a good girl! I will be your mistress, and take care of . . .'

'I say, no!' Lord O'Neill's voice rose. 'You've got it all wrong! Englishmen don't take innocent young girls and . . .'

His voice faltered, remembering the bawdy-houses on the waterfront, the elegant 'establishments' in London, the uninhibited behaviour of the planters in Jamaica.

Opposite him, the dark head was nodding vigorously. 'Oh yes they do! I don't mind, truly. And I will be very *good*, you don't understand how good I can be. Very obedient, and loving, and . . .'

'If you talk like that I shall sell you to someone else,' Lord O'Neill said desperately. 'Look, I'm taking you into a respectable household. Respectable! Do you understand? There is to be no talk of mistresses, or pleasing men . . . it would shock my mother horribly! If you want to be a good girl, then you must work hard at whatever tasks you are set, and speak quietly, and obey the womenfolk in my house. Is that clear, Rachel Blanche Whatever-it-was?'

She dimpled at him. 'Yes, clear. And my name is Rachelle Blanche Nicolette Perigand; but you can call me Peri. Mammy Lucia did, and her family.' She paused, pulling a strand of glossy hair forward and tugging it thoughtfully. 'Then you *truly* did not buy me to be your woman? But that other man said...'

'I heard him. That's why I bought you, to save you from the degradation... Really, Peri, there *are* men in the world who act altruistically, we are not all...'

'What means altruistically? And degred ... degradua...'

Lord O'Neill sighed. He ran his hand through his curly hair, then faced her with a determined look in his eyes. 'Peri, I shall have to tell you the truth. The man who was bidding for you so hotly *did* want you for his woman, I've no doubt of that. And the woman—did you mark her?—runs what is known as a bawdy-house down by the docks. She would have sold your favours to the sailors. I knew that, and I bought you to save you from being...'

He stopped. All the colour and brightness had drained from the small face, and the eyes were fixed with horror, as though they stared at a scene too terrible for him to imagine.

'Peri! What's the matter?'

He leaned forward and took hold of her small hands. Beneath his fingers he could feel her frail bird-bones, the fluttering of a pulse beating wildly in her wrist.

'The sailors came, on the ship,' she said, her voice low. 'They laid on some of the women, though the women did not want them. They cried out and screamed, and there was blood. One woman died, another killed herself. I would die sooner. I would kill myself if they tried ... tried...'

He moved over to sit beside her, putting his arm

round her bare golden shoulders, cuddling her, smoothing the hair back from her brow, talking to her in a low voice to warm some colour back into the pale face, to stop her lips from trembling.

Presently, in the shelter of his arms, she stopped shivering. She looked into his eyes, as anxious as a puppy who knows it has done wrong.

'I thought you would be kind, you see,' she said slowly, 'and gentle. I thought all men... I did not know...'

'Well, you know now,' he said bracingly. 'Nothing horrible will happen to you, I promise. You are safe, and may forget that dreadful ship and the things which took place on board her. You've found a good home.'

The colour, he was relieved to see, was back in her cheeks, the sparkle in her eyes.

'Yes, I shall be safe with you,' she said contentedly. 'If you don't want a mistress, then I will be your servant. I'll please you, I promise. I can do many useful things.' She began to tick her accomplishments off on her fingers, glancing up at him with a trace of anxiety in her clear eyes. 'I can milk a cow, and also a goat. I can make butter and cheese. I weave and sew quite well. Oh, and I can read and write in English very well and in French too.'

He patted her shoulder and stood up, to return to his own seat. 'Well, there you are, then! You are very accomplished, and since I don't need a mistress...'

'You are not ... not *married*, are you?' she asked fearfully.

He laughed out at that and she laughed too, a

gurgle of merriment which he thought enchanting, though he had no intention of telling her so.

'No, I'm not married. Not yet, at any rate. Would it make a difference?'

She tilted her head, considering him, her glance now all mischief, woes forgotten.

'Well, I would be very good to your wife, of course. And to your children. But I'm glad you've not got a woman.'

He drew breath to tell her that while not yet betrothed, he had hopes of being in that happy state shortly, then expelled the breath without speech. After all, why upset her needlessly? He had held back from proposing to Miss Pamela Courtney because he was leaving for the plantations and knew he would be away for several months, and it had not seemed fair to become betrothed when a marriage would be impossible until his return. But now, however, there would be no impediment to a betrothal.

Leaning back at his ease, he watched Peri's wide eyes as the countryside sped past outside, and thought about Pamela. She was a beauty, there was no doubt of that! If she agreed to marry him, he would be the envy of all Liverpool and half London—the male half. She would bring a handsome dowry with her too, and though he did not need the money, it would not come amiss. He thought of the expenses of running his town house, the sums he had lost in the past at White's, Boodle's and Brooks's, the horses he intended to buy. Yes, there was no doubt about it, Pamela's dowry would be put to good use! Also, he had little doubt that she would be an expensive wife. She would set the fashion, entertain royally, and be a credit to him.

'Why do the coach go slow?'

'Why does the coach go slowly,' Lord O'Neill corrected. 'We're nearing the lodge, that's why. I've told the driver to stop for a few moments so that I can go in and explain about you to Pershy.'

The coach stopped as he spoke and Peri, pressing her nose to the glass, saw a neat little house built of red sandstone with a thatched roof and low windows. Lord O'Neill opened the door and jumped down. 'Wait there, Peri,' he commanded, and then he was gone leaving her alone on the leather seat, wondering what 'Pershy' would think of her.

As he had promised he was not gone long and presently he was back and opening the coach door, holding out his hand to her.

'Come along, Peri. Hop down!'

She jumped down and he took her arm, holding it firmly, giving comfort. Then he led her through the low front door and into a cramped, dark parlour, overwarm, with a small, bright-eyed woman in a clean white cap and a dark gown, sitting beside the fire.

She got to her feet, advancing towards them. 'A slave you say, Master Crispin—I *should* say Milord, of course!' she remarked, with the air of one who would continue to call him Master Crispin until her dying day. 'A slave? I don't deny she's almost naked, and her hair's heathenish long, but she's not very black.'

Her voice was so accusing that Peri shrank closer

to his lordship, giving, had she but known it, even more colour to Mrs Pershore's unvoiced suspicions.

'Look, Pershy, you ought to know better, damn it! As if I'd bring my light o' love here! And anyway, she's no more than a child. No, she's just what I said.'

The old woman peered closely into the perplexed, heart-shaped little face. 'Hmm. Well, she's a pretty piece, and might be trained up respectable. But you'll have to dress her decent, Master Crispin, and leave her here for a few days. No use expecting to take her up to the Hall and find her welcomed as a lady's maid immediate, and her with no more idea of how to wait on a young lady than one of those lanky, wicked puppies you were for ever smuggling into the schoolroom, when you were a lad.' She turned to frown into his guiltily grinning face. 'Oh yes, Master Crispin, you may smile, but if you ask me, you bought the lass with no thought whatsoever. Impulsive, that's what. I dare say you'd paid over your blunt before the thought of a present even entered your mind!'

This was so uncomfortably near the truth that his lordship wriggled as guiltily as he had done when discovered in a misdemeanour as a child, then disguised his uneasiness by adjusting his stock and tapping impatient fingers on Mrs Pershore's gleaming dining-table.

'Very well, Pershy, you've had your say. I'll send Martha down to you with some clothing presently.' He turned to Peri, taking one of her hands in a light clasp and speaking seriously. 'You must stay here now, with Mrs Pershore. Soon a servant will bring you some nice clothes and in a day or so, when Mrs Pershore thinks you're ready, you will be able to come up to the Hall and take up your duties.'

Peri glanced doubtfully from his face to the old woman's. 'If you wish it,' she murmured unhappily. 'But you will come back and see me? In these new clothings?'

He thought it best to agree and then, with a final pat on one shoulder, he left the little cottage. The two women heard him climb into the coach, heard the door slam shut and the vehicle move forward. For a moment it seemed as though Peri would follow, for she started towards the door and Mrs Pershore surged forward grimly. But there was no need. Peri's outstretched hand sank to her side. She turned to the nurse and conjured up a wobbly smile.

'He will come back? He won't just ... just leave me?'

The old woman patted her guest's arm. 'Not he! Now then, there's a pallet bed which you may use, and a slip of a room you can have while you're with me. I'll lend you a shawl until Martha arrives with the clothes. Hungry, are you?' She chuckled at Peri's timid nod. 'I thought so! Would you like some new-made bread, with farm butter, and mar-malade?'

'I do not know what mamma-lad is,' Peri said. 'But ... yes, please!'

Chuckling, the old woman led the way out of the parlour and into a tiny kitchen. 'I'll cut the bread, Peri, and you butter it.' She glanced at the girl's golden arms, goosefleshing in the chilly air of the room, and clucked disapprovingly. 'How like the boy to bring you here with scarce a stitch on your back! Wait a minute.'

She left the room and returned with a thick grey shawl which she flung round her guest's shoulders. 'There! That will keep the cold away until your clothing arrives.'

Presently, Mrs Pershore carried the big platter of bread and butter and marmalade back into the parlour, and made tea from the kettle steaming on the hob. The two women sat comfortably beside the fire, sipping the tea and eating. Peri, pulling a face at the hot tea, was, however, enchanted by the marmalade, pronouncing it 'Delicious! Oh, lovely!'

As they ate and drank, Peri's shyness began to evaporate and soon she was chattering away happily, telling Mrs Pershore all about Africa and the village in which she had been brought up. She spoke of her capture and the dreadful journey in the long line of manacled slaves, which twisted and turned through the most remote and uninhabited jungle so that there could be no chance of rescue. But though Mrs Pershore asked, she obeyed his lordship's command to put her voyage out of her mind, and said as little as she could about her time on board the *Snow Tempest*.

Peri, unashamedly greedy, had gobbled the last slice of bread and marmalade, when a sound outside brought her to her feet, to run across to the low, leaded window.

'A coach, like we came in, Pershy,' she exclaimed.

'Big, so *big*, with a coloured picture on the door. But it isn't stopping!'

'Aye, that'll be the O'Neill coat of arms,' Mrs Pershore said. 'Lady O'Neill went out visiting earlier; she'll be getting home in nice time to change for dinner.'

'I didn't see nobody,' Peri said regretfully, returning to her chair. 'But I did see ladies, down at the . . . what's it called? Where the ships are?'

'Down at the docks, child. And I doubt they were ladies,' Mrs Pershore said grimly.

Peri opened her eyes at that. 'Oh, but they *were*! Very fine ladies, wiz . . . with skirts like this!' She held out her arms to their fullest extent. 'And no legs to see at all, but fat white bosoms,' she giggled, indicating her own small breasts, 'All poking out of their gowns. It did look strange!'

'Aye, I dare say. But the fashions worn by those ladies won't be what you'll see 'er ladyship wear, nor what you'll wear yourself,' Mrs Pershore said. 'Now just sit quiet, Peri, while I have another cup of tea. Martha will be here directly, and then you'll be busy enough!'

CHAPTER
TWO

'I won't wear them, I won't! I can't even breathe, so how could I walk? I shall take the horrid things off and wear my nice clean sarong. No, bad Martha, don't dare tie me in!'

Peri, flushed with temper, stood in the small parlour in a print gown, petticoats and woollen stockings, her waist nipped in by stays, her toes cramped into buckled shoes, vainly trying to unfasten the gown while Martha, giggling, tried to tie her calico apron-strings behind.

'Stand still, miss! If you don't wear decent clothes, how do you expect to serve Master Crispin, up at the Hall?' Mrs Pershore demanded, and to her relief Peri stopped scowling and struggling and stood still, wide eyes fixed on the older woman's face.

'Is this true? Would Master Crispin like to see me in these 'orrible clothes?' She shrugged. 'Oh very well, I will keep zem—them—on for a while.'

'I should hope so! And Master Crispin is his lordship to you, miss,' Mrs Pershore retorted heavily. 'Now turn round, slow, so's I can see if you're decent.'

'She ought to wear a cap,' Martha said, putting a hand over her mouth as Peri turned to scowl menacingly at her. 'No really, Peri, I think you should!'

'I won't! My hair is too long and thick to push into an 'orrid cap!'

'Seeing as how she's going to be a lady's maid, she won't be wanting a cap for long,' Mrs Pershore remarked. 'Look at you, Martha!' She sniffed disapprovingly. 'Fine as fivepence in Miss Selina's cast-off gowns and cloaks.'

Martha was a country girl who had known Mrs Pershore since she was old enough to toddle, and bore no grudge for strictures which she knew were true.

''Tis the fashion for lady's maids to dress well,' she said placidly. 'Miss Selina wouldn't want me to go round looking like one of the kitchen servants. But you're right, of course. They'll give Peri nicer clothes than these when she goes up to the Hall. This stuff is Mary's, what she's grown out of.' She eyed Peri curiously. 'How old are you?'

Peri, bending down to straighten her stockings, said, 'I don't know. Fifteen, perhaps?'

'Coo! And Mary's only thirteen. Little, aren't you?'

Peri stood up and eyed the older girl belligerently. 'Yes, perhaps. But I can take care of myself, and so it does not matter! Why, if Mast ... his lordship doesn't like me in these clothes, and I don't see how *anyone* could, then off they come, see?'

'Oh, Gawd!' Martha said, beginning to giggle again. 'Don't you go stripping them clothes off up at the Hall, Peri, no matter what his lordship may say!'

Mrs Pershore, gazing with some apprehension

at her young protégée, seconded this earnestly. 'For if you was to take the clothes off, very likely his lordship would send you packing at once,' she said.

'Oh? He would think it wrong? Then I won't do it. But how can I work in such clothes? And the shoes, how they pinch! Never could I run in them.'

'No, the shoes are too small,' agreed Martha. 'I'll borrow you a better pair, gal, so don't despair. If Mrs Pershore will teach you to curtsy and to speak nice to Miss Selina, I dare say you could come up to the house tomorrow, and then we'll find you a nicer gown.'

Presently, Mrs Pershore despatched her young charge off to bed, with the injunction to go straight to sleep and the morning would come the sooner. Then the two women settled down comfortably in front of the fire for a good gossip.

'She's a nice little thing, though fiery,' Mrs Pershore said, pouring ale into two mugs. 'I thought at first...'

'Aye, so did I,' admitted Martha. 'So young, and half-naked and all! But I take it all's respectable?'

'Naturally.' Mrs Pershore glared. 'As if Master Crispin would bring his light-o'-love back here! He intends her as a present for Miss Courtney. Very respectable.'

'A present? It don't seem right,' Martha said doubtfully. 'Not to give another 'uman being as a present! And you know Miss Courtney, don't you? Peri's a sight too pretty to be welcome, if you get my meaning. Miss Courtney likes to be the one who gets all the attention. She won't want no competition for his lordship's glances.'

While the two heads in the parlour drew closer and the fire roared up merrily and the ale sank in the glasses and was replenished, Peri was tidily shedding her new clothes, tying her sarong round her again, and cuddling into a thick, dark cloak.

So she was to go to bed, was she, whilst Pershy and Martha talked about her and his lordship forgot about her? Oh no! She was Rachelle Perigand, and slave or free, she would do as she liked! She would go up to this hall and see why his lordship had forgotten her. He had promised to come back and see her in the horrid clothes he had chosen for her. Well, he might not see her, but she intended to see him!

Warm and comfortable in the cloak and sarong, her bare feet silent on the matting, Peri crept over to the parlour door and listened.

'There's a bit of a party like, to celebrate his lordship's homecoming,' Martha was saying. 'They'll be dancing and carrying on until the early hours, very like, so I shan't be missed for a while.'

Peri stiffened indignantly. So *that* was why he had not returned to the lodge! He had forgotten his faithful slave in the enjoyment of a party. Nothing, now, would sway her resolve to go up to the Hall and see what his lordship was doing!

Still silent, she padded to the window and eased it open, slipping over the sill and into the trees at the side of the drive, a shadow amongst shadows. She knew she was heading for the house since the coach had disappeared in this direction, and presently she

saw Brownlow Hall for the first time, the carriage
sweep empty but the flambeaux burning merrily on
either side of the front door, showing that the party
was not being held in any of the front rooms.

Accordingly she slid round the side of the house,
hearing music and laughter, smelling perfume and
rich food, flower-scents and candles, so that when
she reached the terrace she had already realised that
the party had spilled out into the night.

There were long windows, flung wide so that
guests could stroll on the illuminated terrace
beneath the coloured lanterns and the light of the
moon above. She crouched behind a bush which
gave her a good view of the proceedings. She could
even see into the long, golden room with its well-
polished floor and little, spindly-legged chairs. An
abundance of handsomely-dressed people still
strolled about inside, despite the fact that most of the
younger people had deserted the ballroom for the
delights of the moonlight and the soft, many-
coloured glow from the lanterns.

Peri's eyes narrowed. Where was he? There were
so many fine gentlemen. But none could be as fine as
his lordship, she was sure.

Then she saw him, strolling from group to group
on the terrace, a curled white wig on his head, tied
back from his face with a black bow at the nape of his
neck. He wore a dark red coat, richly embroidered,
dark breeches, a snowy shirt and stock embellished
with a flashing ruby pin, and pearly stockings. His
shoes were high-heeled, making him look even taller,
and he wore a patch high on one cheek beneath his

blue eye, giving him a quizzical look which Peri much admired.

Then she noticed he was not alone. Catching him up, one small hand placed imperiously upon the sleeve of his coat, was the most dazzling creature Peri had ever seen. Her hair, which was of a shining wheaten gold, fell in a cascade of long curls on to shoulders white as milk, and a heart-shaped patch on her cheek emphasised eyes as blue as cornflowers with long, curling brown lashes. A little cupid-bow mouth was smiling at something his lordship had said, and the hand which was not on his arm kept straying to a delicate diamond necklace around her throat.

While Peri watched, Lord O'Neill tucked the lady's white hand into his elbow, and after a quick glance round, led her down the steps from the terrace, across a short stretch of lawn, and into the darkness of a yew walk. Peri followed them before she had thought, slipping silently over to the stiff and formal yew trees and keeping well back. It was very dark in here, the glow from the lanterns scarcely visible between the trees, but the lady's gown, which was of some white material heavily embroidered at neck and hem with pink and silver flowers, stood out beautifully, as did his lordship's pearly stockings.

Presently, the couple came to a rustic bench standing in an arbor cut into the yew, and Peri, by a dint of silent and rather painful wriggling, managed to squeeze into the arbor close beside the seat. This was better, she thought smugly. She could hear every word the couple uttered, and to be close to his lordship was bliss, even if he was unaware of her presence.

'Miss Courtney! Pamela! I've missed you so much during our long months apart!'

The ardent note in his lordship's voice did not go unnoticed behind the rustic seat, though Miss Courtney appeared unaffected by it.

'Oh nonsense, my lord! You've had plenty to occupy you. Your plantations, the sea voyage, and now the affairs of your house, your sister's wedding—everything. It is I who have been bored, following your sister round Liverpool, buying her wedding finery! *And* the Season's in full swing, too! I'm missing *everything*, just to be present at Selina's nuptials!'

Her voice was cold and clear, with more than a suggestion of pique. Peri, huddled in her hiding place, was chilled by it, but his lordship appeared to notice nothing amiss.

'You've missed me, then? With all your beaux and friends? Yet you truly did miss me?'

'How you do take one up!' Pamela said archly. 'Of course I've missed you in Liverpool, because all my beaux and most of my friends are in London!' She sighed, shivering a little. 'I've had letters, one might almost call them *love*-letters, daily from Sir Roderick Cowper and the Duke of Drysdale, begging me to return to London! Of course I've attended parties and balls here—provincial parties!—and I've been admired, I suppose, but everyone is thinking of Selina all the time. Which is only right and proper, but...'

He caught her hands, saying indulgently, 'But the most beautiful woman in England is not used to taking second place to anyone! My poor darling, how long have you been here?'

Miss Courtney sighed, but did not attempt to remove her hands from his grasp. 'For two whole weeks, my lord! And a country squire—a Mr Wrinstead—dancing attendance on me until I longed to be rude to him. Commonplace creature!'

His lordship laughed softly. 'A country squire! He is the richest man in Lancashire, and very likely in England, too. He's a shipping owner, a landowner, he has cotton mills in the north of the county, coal mines—you name it, Mr Wrinstead's got a finger in the pie. You should be vastly honoured if he danced attendance on you!'

'Oh? He's rich, then?' Miss Courtney's voice became a little more animated. 'Well, he wears the most frightful waistcoats and the rings on his fingers! I made sure they must be paste, for they were so large! Dear me, I hope I didn't snub him!'

'As if you would snub anyone! Adorable creature, tell me you missed me! And then I've a question to ask you ...'

Miss Courtney interrupted him pettishly. 'Not now, my lord, this seat is quite damp.' She had risen to her feet and he followed suit so that they stood facing one another. 'I should like to return to the party now, before we're missed.'

'Oh! But I was going to tell you about the pretty present I've brought you from Jamaica. You'll love it, and it does show you I missed you during the long months of our separation.'

There was a perceptible pause. Miss Courtney, Peri thought crossly, was plainly torn between the desire to save her reputation by a speedy return to the terrace and a wish to find out what her present was to be.

'What is it?' she asked suddenly, drawing closer to him. 'Tell me, Crispin!'

They were standing so close that Peri could not see light between their bodies. She felt unaccountably annoyed, but waited, nevertheless, to hear what else might transpire.

'Well, it's quite small, and very ornamental,' his lordship said, a laugh in his voice. 'But it is useful, too. And . . . you've not got one already!'

'Tell me!' She pulled away from him a little, but his hands reached out and drew her close to him.

'I'll tell you when I've been nicely asked,' he said firmly. And without more ado, he bent his head and kissed Miss Courtney's petal-smooth cheek.

For a moment Miss Courtney resisted, pulling away from his lordship's arms, and then, it seemed, she capitulated. The kisses being rained on her neck and face seemed to touch some answering chord, and she tilted her face to give him her lips. His mouth fastened hungrily upon their softness and Miss Courtney seemed to melt into his arms, giving a soft, dreamy murmur which might almost have been pleasure.

Afterwards Peri told herself virtuously that if only Miss Courtney had continued to resist, all would have been well. But that sudden surrender was too much. Peri caught hold of the hem of Miss Courtney's beautiful skirt and tugged fiercely. Miss Courtney, still locked in his lordship's embrace, neither moved nor spoke. Instead she took a step backwards, still held tightly in his lordship's arms, and the heel of her high, jewelled shoe came down firmly on Peri's hand.

Peri uttered one squeak, then lifted the embroidered hem with her free hand and bit Miss Courtney's leg as hard as ever she could, feeling the silk of her stockings give, satisfyingly, beneath the onslaught of her own sharp and healthy teeth.

At once, there was confusion. Kisses forgotten, Pamela bounded forward, almost driving Peri's hand into the earth, shrieked like a syren, pushed Crispin away and began to sob loudly, clutching her leg, vowing that a wretched little dog had attacked her.

'Crispin, it's all *your* fault! How dare you bring me here and maul me about like a kitchenmaid! And now your wretched dog has bit me to the bone! You should have the brute shot!'

But Crispin, after the first moment of sickening shock when his beloved had torn herself out of his arms shrieking like a mad thing, had seen the small figure scampering away up the yew walk to melt into the hedges as he turned his head.

'No, not a dog. I fancy it was a little cat,' he said, his pensive voice clear and carrying. 'And don't worry, my darling, I'll deal with the creature myself.'

'Shoot it,' Miss Courtney returned vehemently. 'Oh, the pain, Crispin! It's like a knife wound. Help me back to the house.'

'Of course, my own. I'd carry you, but we don't want to risk a scandal. Here, let me put my arm round you. You'd best say you fell on the terrace steps.'

'Certainly not.' Miss Courtney's voice was icily furious. 'I was attacked, Crispin, and you must do something about it.'

'I shall. I'll escort you to the house and then return here.' They were passing the precise spot where the yew hedge was unaccountably darkest. 'I'm sure whatever attacked you will remain just where it is now until my return.' He glanced idly sideways as he spoke. 'Or I really shall be angry.'

Peri, standing miserably in the shadow of the yew hedge, wondered whether it would be worth running back to the lodge, cowering beneath the covers in her bed, and vowing she had never moved from it. But his lordship had not sounded as if his threats were idle. She was sure he had seen her, and anyway one did not lie to the most marvellous person in the world. No, she must wait here and face him when he returned.

He was gone a long time, or so it seemed to Peri, waiting shivering in the shadow of the hedge, all the pleasure of that swift, hard bite gone in apprehension. When his lordship reappeared he carried a lantern and ignored her, making straight for the rustic bench. He sat down upon it and said, without looking towards her, 'Come here.'

She obeyed, moving with lagging steps up the yew walk until she stood in front of him, head hanging.

'What were you doing, spying on Miss Courtney and myself?'

'I was ... you said you'd come and see me in the new clothes, but you didn't, and ... and ...' her voice trailed into silence.

'And why did you bite Miss Courtney in the leg?'

His voice trembled a little as he spoke; with rage, very likely. Peri sighed. She had meant to be so good!

'When you ... when she ... when you ...'

'Don't stammer and stutter, you foolish child. Speak out!'

'When you were cuddling her, she stepped back on to my hand. I'd bit her before I thought!'

He turned his head away for a moment, then faced her once more. In the lamplight his face was stern, as she had never seen it. 'I see. Well, you were spying, were you not? You knew you had no right to follow us into the yew walk.'

She sighed, hanging her head again. 'Yes, I was spying. It was bad,' she admitted contritely. She glanced up, lip trembling. 'Will you beat me?'

He did not answer for a moment, but held out his hand and took hers, turning it to the light so that he could examine the mark where the high heel had bitten into her soft young skin.

She heard the breath hiss through his teeth, then he said, much more gently, 'No, I won't beat you this time. You've been hurt enough. You'll have a nasty bruise there for days, but the skin isn't broken, is it?'

She examined her own hand cursorily. 'I don't think so.' She glanced shamefacedly at him. 'Is the bad thing to bite, or to spy?' she asked at last.

He compressed his lips hard, as though in thought. 'Both,' he said at last. 'Both are very bad, and you deserve to be whipped, but just this once . . .' his voice wavered, and she looked up at him, puzzled. 'Off with you!' he finished abruptly. 'No more spying, and don't you ever *dare* to bite anyone again, or I'll . . .'

He did not finish the sentence but got up and strode back towards the house, the lantern lighting his way.

Peri, making her way mournfully back to the lodge, thought miserably that her temper had let her down. She had known, of course, that to spy was bad, and that to bite was worse. Wrapping her cloak firmly around her and breaking into a trot, she vowed to herself that she would not behave so badly again. Never!

Not that the temptation would ever arise, for she had seen how upset and outraged his lordship had been over her behaviour. As he left her, his shoulders had been shaking! She hoped, remorsefully, that her wickedness had not reduced him to tears.

As she trotted fearlessly through the dark woods back towards the lodge, she thought about the horrible Miss Courtney with her high, cold little voice and that wonderful white-gold hair. How she hated her! But suppose his lordship was really in love with Miss Courtney? Suppose he *married* her?

The dreadful thought stopped her in her tracks for

a moment. Heavens, if he did marry Miss Courtney, she would have to be her servant, as well as his! As she reached the lodge and climbed back into her room, vague thoughts of doing something quite harmless, and not at all bad, to the golden-haired lady were crossing her mind. Something, she told herself, which would discourage Miss Courtney from any thought of becoming his lordship's wife. There were love potions; Mammy Lucia was a great believer in love potions, and if administered correctly, might she not use one of them so that Miss Courtney fell in love with someone other than his lordship? But it was risky, and anyway, Mammy Lucia had given her a love potion to try to make her fall in love with the horrid Portuguese, and all it had done was give her the stomach cramps.

Stomach cramps made her think of wax images. Now that *was* an idea! A pin, stuck in the right place, would give Miss Courtney something to think about other than marriage! And if she was sickly and whining enough, it would doubtless make Lord O'Neill think twice about marrying her, too.

She slipped into bed. In the parlour the low murmur of voices told her that Mrs Pershore and Martha were still chatting, unaware of her exploit.

Peri thought about wax images again. She had a feeling that unless the person being magicked *knew* about the wax image, it might not prove effective. Perhaps it would be more sensible to concoct a poison? Nothing really *bad*, of course. Just a brew which would give Miss Courtney a good turn-out and bring her out in spots. Or there was the one which Mammy Lucia swore by; it brought out one's hair in handfuls, she used to say.

Musing pleasurably upon the prospect of a spotty and balding Miss Courtney being spurned by his lordship in favour of herself, Peri fell quickly, and happily, asleep.

And Lord O'Neill, reaching the safety of his own room, closed the door, doused the lantern, and then gave vent to his bottled-up mirth. What an impulsive, wicked child she was, his Peri! And how he would enjoy seeing her crestfallen face when he handed her over to Pamela in the morning, as his present brought all the way from Jamaica. It would serve her right, the ... the little cat!

He had been sorry for Pamela's fright and the pain of the bite, of course. But it had, in truth, been the tiniest of wounds, the skin had been no more than bruised. And his slave-child had been painfully trodden on!

He grinned to himself, peeling off his coat and beginning to unbutton his frilled shirt. For all her faults, Peri was a sweet little creature. Passionate, too, or he was no judge of women. But she would curb her feelings once she was Pamela's maid, and no doubt when she was the recipient of his darling's tender warmth, she would transfer the affection she at present felt for himself to her new owner.

He took off his wig and scratched his head. Yes, there was no doubt about it, Pamela could charm the birds off the trees. She was a diamond of the first water. He only had to think of the pale gold curls, the white skin, the enormous, pale blue eyes, to feel a

stirring within him. He knew she would accept his
suit. And while she was under his roof he would be
able to admire her, and watch that Peri behaved
herself, learning the ways of an English household.

If he could have known the thoughts which were
running so pleasantly through Peri's mind, he would
not have dropped off to sleep quite so quickly. Nor
slept so dreamlessly!

CHAPTER
THREE

As it happened, his lordship's present-giving ceremony had to be put off for a few days, due to the fact
that one of his boxes, the one containing Lady
O'Neill's china, had been stowed away in the very
bottom of the hold and could not be retrieved until
the hold was emptied. So in the circumstances his
lordship put off bringing Peri up to the Hall until
such time as all his gifts could be assembled.

To punish her for the incident in the yew walk he
did not visit the lodge the following day. However, he
was not a man to brood upon things, and the day
after that saw him striding into the lodge, to kiss Mrs
Pershore's cheek and ask for his slave.

Peri came into the parlour and sank into a deep
curtsy, her eyes lowered. She was wearing the new
clothes which Martha had brought, a pink gingham
dress, full in the skirt and low in the bodice, but with
a white kerchief demurely folded in the neck to hide
her low décolletage. Her hair had been brushed until
it shone and confined in a knot on top of her head,
with three curls hanging down to bob when she
moved.

Lord O'Neill took in her appearance with
appreciation, spiced, it must be admitted, with
pique. Why did she not look up at him with those
great, worshipping eyes?

'You look delightful,' he said however, quickly amending it to, 'Most suitable'. She smiled, flicked him a quick glance, then her attention returned to the floor at his feet once more.

'Yes, I do look nice,' she agreed sunnily. 'But I *hate* stays, they push my breasts up so they show and then Mrs Pershore makes me cover them with a handkerchief! I don't see the sense of it!'

Eyeing the swell of her breasts beneath the white kerchief, his lordship quite agreed with her, but said soothingly, 'Stays are very fashionable, and so is a low décolletage. I dare say, however, that Mrs Pershore thinks you a trifle young to show off your . . . er . . . figure.'

'What means figure?'

His lordship grinned. The meekness and conformity were only skin deep, evidently. 'In this instance, it means breasts,' he said bluntly. 'You must watch your words, Peri! In polite society the parts of the body are not mentioned quite so . . . so frankly.'

'By me they are,' Peri said positively. 'Otherwise how am I to say what I think? But Mrs Pershore says I'll quickly learn to please.' She glanced at him fleetingly through her thick lashes. 'Not *men*,' she added, in case he had misunderstood her. 'Mrs Pershore doesn't want me to please men, she wants me to please the ladies of your house.'

'Well, you certainly curtsy beautifully,' he said encouragingly. He patted her head, wanting to see the frank glance return to his face, but she kept her eyes resolutely lowered. Losing patience, he said sharply, 'For God's sake look at me when I'm speaking to you! What's the matter?'

Startled, the big eyes flew to his face. 'But how is this? Mrs Pershore said to keep my eyes lowered, and not to stare so!'

His lordship sighed. 'Oh, dear! Perhaps she's right, I don't know, I don't look at the servants, I suppose. But however you may behave to the ladies, you'll look at *me*, do you understand? I like to know what you're thinking, and I can't do that if all I can see is the top of your head!'

'Good!' Peri said gleefully. 'I shall tell Mrs Pershore she's wrong! I think it is ... oh, what's the word? ... I know, *sly*, to keep one's eyes lowered all the time.'

'Don't be so frank, child,' his lordship said nervously. 'You don't want to hurt Mrs Pershore's feelings, do you? Just behave prettily and do as you're told at once, and you won't go far wrong. I wonder why she thought it best for you to keep your eyes lowered?'

Mrs Pershore, entering the room at that moment, said shortly, 'Be off with you, Peri, I want a word with his lordship. Go and finish the washing in the kitchen, if you please.'

Peri obediently trotted out, closing the door behind her, and Lord O'Neill found himself facing his old nurse across the parlour.

'Well, Pershy? Why the lowered eyes and clasped hands?'

'Master Crispin, that little creature you bought ... well, she's a taking little soul, there's no doubt of that. She means no harm, but if she goes up to the house and ... and someone puts her into low-cut, fashionable clothes, and she goes round giving men that ... that *look*, she'll be seduced before a week's out! Your cousin Jerome arrived last night, didn't he? How do you think he'll behave if she gives him one of those flirtatious, sparkling looks? She's got to be protected from herself, sir!'

'Yes, I see what you mean. But when she meets Jerome, the last place her eyes should be is on the ground! Nor she won't want her hands clasped, neither,' he added in a burst of frankness.

Mrs Pershore sniffed. 'Master Jerome was always a handful,' she said disapprovingly. 'Now he fancies himself as a rake, a bruising rider, a sporting man and goodness knows what beside. If he takes a fancy to your slave, Master Crispin, I wouldn't give *that* for her chances.' She snapped her fingers in the air, her expression eloquent.

'I never thought,' his lordship admitted. 'I'll *tell* Jerome she's just an innocent child, but...'

'He's been paying Miss Courtney a lot of attention, mind,' Mrs Pershore interrupted reflectively. 'If you are really going to give Peri to her, there's your problem solved. You won't find Master Jerome blotting his copybook by chasing Miss Courtney's servant.' She glanced reflectively at his lordship's expressive face. 'Miss Courtney's got a nice dowry and she'll inherit when her Papa dies, her being the only child. I dare say your cousin bears that in mind, as well as her pretty looks.'

'Oh! She didn't mention ... but there, that's of no

importance ... and I certainly *am* going to give the child to Pam ... Miss Courtney. She'll love her! And, as you say, she'll take better care of her than ever I could!'

'I didn't say that, exactly,' Mrs Pershore said. 'But there, Master Crispin, be off with you now. You've seen the girl respectably dressed, and I've still got plenty to teach her. Presently Martha and Polly are coming down here. They'll be heads for us.'

'Heads? How sinister that sounds! I trust Peri hasn't been instructing you, Pershy, in head-hunting!'

'For shame, Master Crispin! No, Martha and Polly are going to let me show Peri how to dress their hair fashionable. Now be off with you, for we've work to do if you have not.'

Peri, who had been crouching outside the door trying to listen to their low-voiced conversation, scampered across the kitchen and began energetically washing a fine wool shawl, giving the impression, she sincerely hoped, that she had been so engaged for some time. To her disappointment, his lordship left the house without seeing her again, but by a dint of peering through the low little window she saw the top of his fair head as it disappeared round the end of the garden wall.

Presently Martha and Polly, giggling mightily, came and delivered their heads to Mrs Pershore's tender mercies, and then to Peri's inexpert hands. But Peri was a clever girl with a natural flair for coaxing hair into curls, so that when the two maids returned to the Hall, each was secretly well satisfied with the new style she had been given. Polly's thin, mousy hair had been curled and piled on rolls of horsehair to give it added height and the illusion of thickness. Martha, whose rich brown locks needed no such artifice, rejoiced in a mass of curls at both sides of her face, and a neatly curled fringe across her forehead. The back hair, brushed and pomaded, was curled into a bun and tied in place with green ribbon.

'I did well, yes?' Peri asked wistfully, watching the two girls make their way up towards the big house. 'They liked their curls, no?'

'You did very well,' Mrs Pershore agreed warmly. She believed in giving praise where it was due. 'And now I want to see you iron that petticoat, the one you washed this morning.'

'Suppose I too hot make the iron?' Peri enquired mournfully. She had already tried her hand at ironing and found it dull work, tiring and fraught with danger, for her tendency to dream and allow the heavy weight of the iron to linger over elaborate ruchings had already caused the death by burning of his lordship's finest nightshirt.

'Come along, miss,' Mrs Pershore said firmly. She had noticed that Peri's English grew rapidly worse when she was bored or annoyed, and had been a children's nurse for too long not to recognise excuses when she heard them. 'I don't say ironing is fun, mind, but you'll do plenty of it when you're working as a lady's maid. Now remember what I told you, keep your mind on your work and keep your iron moving.' To try to bribe her charge a little she added, 'And when the petticoat looks just as it ought, we'll have a nice cup of tea and a piece of pigeon pie.'

It took a long time to iron a petticoat well enough to please Mrs Pershore. She had a supply of the wretched things, Peri realised, in a big laundry basket in the lean-to shed by the back door, and every time Peri made a mistake, crushing lace or marking the delicate fabric, Mrs Pershore would cry, 'Never mind, gal, leave that. Let's try another one!'

Indeed, when the eleventh petticoat turned out beautifully, and Peri thankfully stood the heavy iron back in the hearth, she was compelled to say impulsively, 'How I hate to iron! I think I would almost rather go to the sailors!'

Mrs Pershore turned and gave her a furious glare. 'I shall pretend I didn't hear that remark, miss! Much you know about it! You've no more idea what it means than a new-born lamb. And unless you want to iron *twenty* petticoats, you'd best not say it again. The idea! Now sit yourself down and we'll have that pie!'

She produced the pigeon pie from the pantry and cut two generous slices, then heaped pickles on the plates, cut bread and butter, and poured the hissing water into the pot. Peri, always appreciative of good food, squared her elbows and tucked in. And presently, when her plate was clean, she ran round the table and hugged her hostess.

'You are so good,' she said remorsefully, 'and I am

so bad! I *do* hate to iron, but for you I don't mind. There!'

The meal thus ending so amicably, the two of them cleared away and washed up and then Mrs Pershore announced her intention of going to visit her friend Mrs Twining, the keeper's wife, in her cottage on the estate.

'You can come too, Peri, or you can stay here,' she offered, putting a shawl round her shoulders. 'Mrs Twining's a kind soul, she'll find something to keep you amused.'

Peri, with her sweetest smile, declined the treat, however. 'I'll sit by the fire and mend the lace on his lordship's nightshirt,' she offered. 'If I cut out the big burnt bit I'm sure he'll never notice.'

'Very well, my dear. If I'm late, just you go off to bed.'

But as soon as her mentor had disappeared down the drive, off came Peri's shoes and stockings and on went the dark cloak. She slipped out into the cool evening, sniffing the fresh scents appreciatively. She made for the house, then stopped at the edge of the drive to consider.

It was unlikely that another party was being held, and probably unlikely too, that she would be fortunate enough to glimpse his lordship. Why should she not explore the outbuildings and the gardens, however? She realised that she had not the faintest idea of her surroundings; all she had seen was the back of the big house, the terrace and the yew walk. And the lodge and its small vegetable garden, of course.

Accordingly, she made her way round to where

she could see outbuildings, dark against the starlit sky. She went cautiously, slipping silently from shadow to shadow. Once a dog ran barking out of a shed, but she went boldly up to him, talking to him as she might have done to an over-adventurous child, and he licked her hands and then trotted quietly behind her as she continued her tour of inspection.

She crossed a wide, cobbled yard and sniffed. Horses, their warm bodies scenting the air and mingling with the farmyard smells of hay, straw and manure. She found a door, opened it, and slipped inside. She had always loved horses, and wanted to see these more closely.

She began to prowl up the stalls, peering at their occupants in the dimness. Her eyesight was excellent, and she could see quite well in the stables despite the gloom, but as she traversed the length of the place, she became aware that, from the end stall, a faint light was emanating. Curious, she crept softly towards the source of the light and with infinite patience, peered round the end of the stall.

A handsome mare stood there on three legs, while a fourth was held up to the ministrations of a dark-haired young man who must be, Peri supposed, a few years older than Lord O'Neill. He was wearing a frilled shirt, open at the neck, and dark breeches, but at one side of the stall he had flung down a deep blue coat with buttoned-back lapels and a lace stock.

He appeared to be applying a fomentation to the mare's leg, for close by stood a steaming pail with some sort of poultice in it. The man was scooping handfuls of the nauseous mixture out of the bucket and slapping it on to the mare's leg, and presently he reached for a strip of bandage and began to try to wrap it round the wound, or boil, or whatever he was treating. The mare, however, had different ideas. She whinnied shrilly, moved her hindquarters restively, and planted a hoof firmly on the man's toe.

He exclaimed sharply, following this with several expletives which Peri had frequently heard on the sailors' lips and impulsively she ran forward, pushing against the mare's rump, saying soothingly, 'I will hold her, sir, while you put on the bandage.'

Dark eyes studied her appreciatively, and a grin stole across the man's hard, handsome countenance. 'Will you, by God? And where have you sprung from, you pretty piece?'

'From Mrs Pershore's cottage, where I am staying at present,' Peri replied innocently. She leaned against the mare's smooth chestnut rump to keep the animal from turning again. 'Who are you, sir, and where do you come from?'

He was tying the bandage into a neat knot, and when he had finished he put the leg down on the ground again and turned to survey his companion. He had a dark, dare-devil face, a sensuous mouth, and laughter lurked now in his heavily-lidded eyes.

'I am Jerome Harcourt, Miss Pershore, if you're any the wiser. I've come to the hall to see my pretty cousin wed her dull bridegroom.'

Peri put her hand to her mouth and giggled. 'I'm not Miss Pershore! I'm . . . just staying with her. I'm Peri.'

'Peri? That's a funny little name.' He strolled

across to her in a couple of strides and stood over her, taller than any man she had previously known, a lock of dark hair flopping across his forehead, a look on his face which she neither understood nor wished to interpret. Two lean, muscled hands caught her shoulders in a grip which she knew instinctively would be impossible for her small strength to resist.

'Peri,' he said again, softly. 'What a funny little name!'

She stood still between his hands, looking up into his face, her eyes wide with innocent enquiry. 'It is not *all* my name,' she was beginning, when, without warning, she saw the face above her darken, the nostrils flare, and then he bent his head and fastened his lips on her mouth, dragging her into a hard and ruthless embrace.

Fear burst like a soft bombshell in her stomach. He must have felt her instinctive flinch away from him but he took no notice, his mouth working on hers until he parted the soft lips, ignoring her whimpering, the hammering of her heart, her wild, fruitless efforts to evade him. She jerked her head back from his for a second, felt his hard hands move slowly over her back as his mouth came down over hers once more.

And then, with all the strength at her command, Peri kicked out at his shins. She stamped on his feet with her bare toes, she twisted like an eel in his arms. He gave a muffled laugh and caught hold of a handful of her abundant hair. 'What's in a kiss?' he said breathlessly. 'No harm, pretty Peri! And I'll take another for your daring to fight me!'

She gave a choked scream—and suddenly, she was free of him. He was sprawling against the side of the stall, his expression ugly, and she was pushed back against the other wall, forgotten.

Lord O'Neill stood over his cousin, his fists clenched, his face every bit as furious as the other man's.

'Jerome, get to your feet and I'll knock your teeth down your throat,' he growled. 'What the hell do you think you're doing, seducing my servants in my stables?'

Jerome scrambled to his feet, a rueful grin on his countenance. He did not so much as glance at Peri, trembling against the opposite wall. 'How fierce you are, cousin! But don't let's fight over the child! She's a pretty piece, and all I was doing was kissing her! By God, don't say you've never done so yourself?'

'No. I don't seduce children,' Lord O'Neill said briefly, the ice still in his voice. 'And nor will you, Jerome, while you're under my roof. Leave Peri alone! Is that clear?'

'As crystal,' drawled Jerome. He bent and picked up his coat and stock, and began struggling into both. 'I've seen to the mare's leg, so I'll go back to the house now.'

Peri, still leaning against the wall, watched as he moved the bucket out of reach of the mare's hooves, flung a blanket across her back, and then strolled out of the stable without a backward glance. Once at the door, however, he suddenly remarked, 'She's your fancy piece, is she then, Cris? I don't blame you, but whatever will Pamela say when I tell her?'

'What would she say if I told her I caught you trying to seduce a maidservant?' countered his lordship evenly. 'Really, Jerome, I thought better of you.'

The other man's face appeared round the stable door. He was grinning. 'Oh, to hell with it, Crispin, I behaved like a dog! I'm sorry, damn it, and you made me feel a great fool. But I've been dancing attendance on Pamela without so much as glancing at another woman for weeks, and ...' His eyes slid over Peri's small, trembling figure. 'It was too bad, and I'm sorry. There!'

Both men laughed, Crispin saying easily, 'All's forgotten, Jerry,' and then the couple in the stable heard the other man's feet retreating across the stableyard.

When he was sure they were alone, Crispin went over to Peri and tilted her chin to make her look into his face.

'Still frightened, chick? My cousin is no end of a fellow, but I think he would stop short at rape! He scared you, didn't he?'

Dumbly, Peri nodded, her eyes big with tears.

'Well now, it might have been worse, and it will teach you a lesson! You're much too pretty to go wandering around alone at night. You might have been discovered by someone far less easy to discourage than my cousin Jerome!' She remained looking up at him, the tears overflowing now and running slowly past her trembling mouth. He caught her shoulders, holding her gently, his voice suddenly sharp. 'What did he do to you? *Was* it only a kiss?'

She kept her eyes fixed on his, but colour bloomed in her cheeks. 'He ... he made ...' she faltered.

'What? What did he make you do?'

His mouth had a white line round it, his eyes were chips of ice.

The small face so close to his own crumpled. 'He made me open my mouth,' she said, beginning to sob.

He held her close, letting the tears soak into his coat and the tension gradually leave her body as the hiccuping sobs lessened. She felt his hand, gently smoothing her dishevelled hair, for his cousin's ministrations had brought her bun tumbling down her back.

Gently, his hands still soothing, his body warm and undemanding, he said, 'Peri, my dear child, that is ... can be ... part of a kiss. It's quite all right! You're all right!'

'Oh,' she said forlornly. 'I feel ... broken.'

His arms tightened for a minute, then he held her back from him, his eyes roving across her. The kerchief had gone in the struggle and her small breasts showed provocatively above the top of her dress. Her mouth was pink and swollen from Jerome's kisses, and her eyes, tear-wet still, gazed adoringly up into his.

Lord O'Neill swallowed, aware of a wild, mad desire to sweep the child into his arms and show her what lovemaking was all about. But being in love with Pamela, he told himself firmly, must make such temptation ridiculous. Peri was a little slave-girl, and it was his duty to take care of her, not to ... to ...

He smiled at her bracingly instead. 'You're not broken at all,' he assured her. 'Just a little tumbled and ruffled, and justifiably annoyed with my cousin Jerome. Now I'll take you back to the lodge, and you must go to bed and forget all about it. Except that, in future, you'll remain with Mrs Pershore at nights until you come up to the Hall to live, and then you'll shut yourself into your own room, and lock the door.'

He walked her back to the lodge, and by the time she stood outside her own window once more, Peri had regained command of herself. She said shyly to his lordship, 'That's the second time you've rescued me! But I'm all right now, truly I am.' She glanced anxiously at his face in the faint starlight. 'It was only a small thing, that ... kiss?'

'Only a small thing, and one which will not occur again,' he promised her. 'Now hurry back into your room and cuddle down. You'll be coming up to the Hall in the morning!'

'Come along, Peri, don't be shy. What's happening is that the master has got all his stuff what he brought back from Jamaica set out in the picture gallery. Ooh, loads of lovely things, there is! And he wants you there because he brought you back too, in a way. He'll tell Lady O'Neill about you, and she'll tell you where you are to sleep and what your duties are, and so on.'

Mrs Pershore had been firm in her resolve that Peri was not to be told she was to be a present for anyone.

'She's that fond of Master Crispin she might just light out,' she said. 'Anyway, there's no saying ... Silence is golden, see, Martha?'

Now, walking in through the front door into a marble-floored hall decorated with dark old portraits and two immense suits of armour, Peri said stoutly above the beating of her heart, 'I am not afraid. Why should I be? No one knows it was me burned the nightshirt, nor do they know about the petticoats.'

Martha gave her a puzzled look, but before she could ask any questions they were at the door of the picture-gallery where servants and family already occupied quite a third of the enormous room.

Peri hung back for a moment, shy of so many eyes, until Lord O'Neill, standing beside an impressive pile of presents, saw her and came across to her. Taking her wrist, he led her over to the presents.

'Look, Peri, these are gifts for my family and the servants. I will tell you each person, and you will carry the object across to them. Curtsy when you hand it over, and then come back to me. Is that clear?'

Peri nodded, but said anxiously, 'How shall I know who is who?'

'Oh, I've told them to stand up and step forward when their name is called. Except for my Mama, Lady O'Neill, who is the white-haired lady sitting on the blue velvet chair. Can you manage?'

'Yes, I think so.' But he could tell by the way her eyes lingered doubtfully on his face that there was another question to come. 'Your c-cousin, sir? Will I have to take him a gift?'

Lord O'Neill smiled at her. 'Yes, Peri,' he returned gently, 'but he's ashamed of his behaviour, and won't bite you. Not in front of all these people, anyway! You mustn't be afraid of him.'

Before his eyes, the sparkling, affectionate child changed into an outraged young lady.

'Afraid? Of *him*?' She almost spat out the words, drawing herself up to her full small height. 'I'm not afraid of *anyone*!'

'Good. Now the first present is this carving. For my sister, Miss Eleanor.'

Peri snatched the carving from him, whipped across the room and almost flung it into his younger sister's lap. Eleanor, startled, thanked her brother and eyed Peri with considerable perplexity; a perplexity which was echoed in several of the faces surrounding her.

However, after her one spurt of temper, Peri behaved beautifully, presenting each gift with a deep curtsy and an upward glance out of her mischievously sparkling eyes which brought her kind smiles from the older people and appreciative glances from the young menservants.

Only to Jerome did she present a wooden and unsmiling countenance. Even Miss Courtney, receiving a tropical shell, an elephant carved out of ivory and a fan made of peacock feathers, was handed her gifts with a smile.

At last all the smaller presents had been given. The servants, well satisfied, were examining their trophies. Lord O'Neill glanced at the boxes still waiting to be distributed. Selina's pearls, his mother's china—and Peri.

The china was too much for the girl's strength, so a footman carried it over to Lady O'Neill, who received it with great joy. She began to unpack it at once, exclaiming over every shell-like piece, and while she did so Lord O'Neill's eyes were irresistibly drawn to Miss Courtney's pale, patrician countenance.

She was looking at Peri, and on her face was an expression so cold, and at the same time so full of revulsion, that it made him shiver. Dear God, Pershy was right, he thought wildly. Pamela doesn't like slaves!

And then his mother put down the last piece of china and all eyes swung expectantly back to him once more. He took a deep breath and put his hand on Peri's shoulder. It felt very small and frail beneath his fingers and he felt her give a little shiver and draw closer to him. It aroused all his protective instincts and unconsciously he moved his fingers in a small, soothing motion, kneading her flesh through the pink gingham.

'I expect you are wondering what this little creature is doing here,' he began. 'She has a very long French name indeed, but in truth she is Peri, a slave who has come all the way from Africa. And she's a present . . .' His mouth felt dry, and he saw a look flicker across Pamela's face which filled him with deeper dismay; an acquisitive look, almost cruel.

'A present for someone very dear to me,' his voice

went on. 'Selina, my dear sister, I have brought you a companion, a servant, and, I hope, a friend.' He squeezed Peri's shoulder. 'Your final task, Peri, is to take yourself over to my sister, Miss Selina, so soon to be Mrs Tufton Mapp.'

As the girl crossed the room his lordship saw a very thoughtful expression flit across his mother's beautiful, serene face, but she smiled warmly at Peri and stretched out her hand to the girl.

'What a lovely surprise!' Selina said placidly. She was, in fact, horrified, but was far too well brought up to embarrass either a servant or her brother by showing her feelings. 'I am sure Peri will be a very good servant, and we shall be happy together. Thank you, my dear brother.'

'She's a good girl,' Lord O'Neill offered a trifle nervously. 'And now for my final gift.' He lifted the necklace out of its soft bed of cotton floss and saw Pamela's eyes glow as they fell on the perfectly matched, softly gleaming pearls.

'Pearls for a pearl,' his lordship said ardently, passing the long box over to her.

With the last of the presents distributed, the party began to break up. Only Peri stood awkwardly by Selina's side, not knowing what to do or where to go.

But Selina was a good-hearted girl, and took her new servant by the hand, leading her out of the picture-gallery and across the hall towards the stairs, chattering all the while.

'I've got a lady's maid, of course; Martha. But no doubt you'll be able to help her. Anyway, I'll take you up to my room and show you where you will sleep and what your tasks will be.' Turning, she added over her shoulder to someone mounting the stairs behind them, 'Truly, Pamela, Crispin is the most thoughtful of brothers! I'd never have thought of getting a lady's maid from Jamaica!'

Peri, glancing curiously back, saw the light blue eyes fixed on her malevolently, the pink mouth pulled into an expression of distaste.

'Why should you, Selina? God knows, you could get yourself a little girl from the poorhouse for a few shillings a week. Slaves cost the earth. But then you've complete control over them.' She paused, the blue eyes sliding over Peri's slender figure. 'Yes, a slave. One would control her, body and soul.'

Selina returned no answer to that but opening a door, pulled Peri gently inside, shut it, and stood staring helplessly at the younger girl.

Peri, staring back with unabashed curiosity, saw that Selina was really very like her brother, with the same brilliant blue eyes and crisply curling fair hair. But she was a trifle plump, her expression easy-going, her voice and demeanour placid. She completely lacked her brother's forcefulness or decisiveness.

'You do speak English, don't you, Peri? Oh dear me, whatever was my brother thinking of? I didn't say so before Pamela—Miss Courtney—I've been training Martha to lady's-maid me for months now, and I'm quite content with her. Not that I'm not pleased with you, except that ...' She stopped speaking, and regarded Peri steadily for a moment; then a light dawned in her eyes. 'I know how it was! He meant you for Pamela! Of course, with her passion for something different, a slave would have seemed the very thing.'

Peri said nothing, but continued to stare with great interest at the other girl. 'Yes and then, of course, he realised that it would never *do*,' Selina went on. 'Oh, I know she and I have been friends since childhood, but that's more habit than anything. I wouldn't give Pamela a lap-dog I was fond of, let alone a mere child.'

Peri found her tongue at last. 'I am not a mere child! I am probably quite fifteen. And what did you mean, he meant me for Pamela? He gave me to *you*! I don't understand!'

'Oh, nothing,' Selina said hastily. 'And there'll be plenty that you can do for me with my wedding so close. The only thing is, when I go away to London I don't see ... But there, that's a problem for later. The problem for now is where shall you sleep, for Martha has a bed in my dressing-room. Oh, I suppose you can sleep in the attics, with the other servants. How would that be?'

'I don't know what means attics,' Peri said forlornly. She bit her lip, then smiled, trying to look bright and helpful. 'But I'll do whatever you say, Miss Selina. His lordship said I was to please his ladies.'

'Yes, and I mean to have a word with his lordship later,' Selina said ominously. 'And for now, you may busy yourself with some light work. I've got a dress with a great rent in the hem which you could stitch. Or how about some ironing?'

And to her dismay, Peri found herself being instructed in the art of heating the iron, whilst her new mistress selected a small pile of handkerchiefs and ruffs 'for you to practise on', as she kindly put it.

Having seen her new acquisition started on her task, Selina left the room and went in search of her mother, to lay before her the puzzle of Peri's sudden appearance among them. She paused in the doorway, hearing Peri mutter something, then left, wondering whatever the words could have meant.

'It sounded like "I'd much rather sailors",' she disclosed when she eventually ran her mother to earth. 'But it could not have been, of course!'

CHAPTER
FOUR

WITH the wedding only three days away the house resembled nothing so much as the backstage area of a London theatre just before a performance. There seemed to be women everywhere, thought his lordship, for Pamela and Eleanor were not to be the only bridal attendants. Two young cousins, Louisa and Charlotte, were to be bridesmaids also, and they and their proud mamas were already in residence.

Tonight there was to be a formal dinner at which Selina's husband-to-be, Tufton Mapp, would be introduced to all the neighbouring gentry. The only bright spot was that a quartet had been engaged, so that after they had dined, the younger members of the party might indulge in dancing. At least it might mean that he would get Pamela to himself for half an hour, his lordship thought hopefully.

His sister had been very nice about her present, but had left him in little doubt that, charmed though she had been to receive Peri, his gift was nevertheless something of an embarrassment to her.

'She would probably make a much better lady's maid than Martha,' she told him, 'but I couldn't possibly let Martha see that! I can find Peri work, of course, especially with the wedding so close, and I can take her to London with me. But not as a lady's maid.'

'No? Well, you'll doubtless find her something to do,' his lordship had returned easily. 'She wants to please you, I'm sure.'

'For now, she can assist Martha,' Selina had replied. 'I'll be quite happy, in fact, to train her for six months so that she can be given to Eleanor. After all, our sister is nearly sixteen and will soon be wanting a maid of her own.'

In this manner both brother and sister were satisfied, except that when Lord O'Neill thought it over, he had felt constrained to go round to the biggest jewellers in Liverpool and buy a string of pearls which, if possible, were even more beautiful than those he had recklessly presented to Miss Courtney. Selina, receiving them with delight, announced that he was a darling, adding impulsively that whoever married him would be the luckiest female alive. Lord O'Neill, regarding the sizeable sums which he had lately spent on pearls and Peri, was beginning to think himself recklessly extravagant, but Selina's words did much to restore his self-esteem. After all, he wanted to be a good brother to both his sisters, and it seemed he had been!

So now, in all the glories of midnight blue brocade lavishly embroidered with silver thread, the coat thrown open to reveal a waistcoat whose gilt buttons were the size of guinea pieces, Lord O'Neill walked along the upper hall towards Jerome's room.

He tapped on the door and walked in, to find his

cousin formally attired in dark brown velvet with creamy lace at throat and wrists, his high-heeled, silver-buckled shoes adding to his already considerable height. He had powdered his hair, and this made his face seem even darker and more dangerous by comparison with the whitened curls.

'Ready, Jer? I'm not going down into that gaggle of females without some male support!'

Jerome grinned. 'Yes, your mamma has certainly provided a quantity of females, but don't fear, I'll support you. In fact I'm not afraid of women, it's ladies I run shy of! And by that token, where's Peri? I've scarcely seen her since you handed her to Selina in the picture-gallery.'

'A good thing too! What do you want with her? Have you no mistress in keeping?'

'Steady, Cris!' Jerome's deep voice sounded amused. 'In fact, I've not. I have a preference for married women. They are more ... experienced in the arts of dalliance, and less expensive. Peri, however, is different.'

'Peri seems to have developed a distaste for you. She steers clear of you, I imagine.'

Jerome adjusted his falls of lace, glanced once more in the mirror, and then strolled across and linked arms with his lordship.

'*Does* she?' he said softly. 'Well, well! I do trust, my dear cousin, that she's not been told I'm a seducer of innocents?'

'Not by me,' Lord O'Neill responded. 'Your reputation is for livelier prey. You were more than friends with Lady Fitzgerald, I believe, and Maria Hughes's latest brat is said to be in your image. I would have thought Peri not your style at all!'

They were in the corridor now, strolling towards the wide staircase.

'All true, alas,' Jerome sighed. 'The truth is, Cris, that I'm looking for a wife. And ladies, my dear coz, can be damned strange about mistresses! In a word, I've been advised that if I want to spread my ... er ... attentions around, I must leave ladies of quality alone.' He sighed, beginning to descend the stairs. 'There are, of course, charming and accomplished courtesans who would be delighted to accommodate me. But I've a great fancy for your little Peri; she's quite charming, you know. I'm not particularly eager to throw my money about, but I'd be happy to buy her from you for whatever you paid, and I'd keep her in luxury, I promise you that!'

'Until you grew tired of her.' Lord O'Neill's blue eyes chilled. 'She's only a child, Jer, scarcely fifteen! And anyway, she belongs to Selina, who most certainly won't sell her to you.'

'Not even if Peri wanted to come to London with me? I've a notion,' Jerome said softly, 'that once I'd breached her defences, she'd not be unwilling.'

'Jerome, if you dare ...' Lord O'Neill was beginning, equally softly, when they were interrupted.

'Good evening, sirs! And which of you is going to take me in to dinner?'

Miss Courtney, fine eyes shining, lips curved into an exquisite smile, stood before them. From one mind, at least, Peri's importance faded.

'Miss Courtney, as your host I must claim the honour!'

Selina, watching the little scene, saw Miss Courtney, with a dazzling smile, rest one white hand on her brother's arm and walk away with him. But she did not fail to notice the glance which Miss Courtney allowed to slide over Jerome, taking in the broad shoulders, the hard, rakish face, the gleam in his dark eyes.

'Did you see Miss Courtney's expression then, Tufton?' Selina whispered, clutching Mr Mapp's arm. 'I do believe that if my cousin Jerome had thirty thousand a year instead of a monstrous pile of debts, she'd have him!'

The party was over. Despite her tasks Peri had made it her business to watch his lordship for quite half an hour, and had the doubtful pleasure of seeing him dancing with Miss Courtney, fetching a glass of orgeat for Miss Courtney, and flirting with Miss Courtney. It was, accordingly, in no very happy frame of mind that she re-entered her young mistress's bedroom later that night, since it was her turn to help Miss Selina out of her finery and into bed.

Outside she could hear the clatter of departing guests, and knew that Selina would not be up until the last coach had departed, so she began, leisurely, to make ready.

The bed had been warmed, but she turned the covers down and laid out Selina's frilly nightgown before the fire, close enough so that the flames would warm, but not scorch, the fine lawn. She went into the powdering closet and checked that the gown which would protect her mistress's person from the dust when the powder was brushed out of her hair was hanging on its hook, and that the brushes were cleaned and ready. Next she brushed out the skirts of the elegant green sack-gown which Selina would wear around the house next day, and laid out a selection of ribbons.

When she heard the door opening behind her she picked up the jug of milk which stood ready, prepared to pour it into the pan and heat it on the hob, for Miss Selina always had a glass of hot milk before retiring. But to her surprise it was Mr Mapp who came towards her, holding out Selina's peacock-feather fan.

'Yes, sir?' She smiled tentatively at her mistress's betrothed. 'Miss Selina is still saying goodbye to her guests. Can I help you?'

Mr Mapp was a sturdy, sensible man past the first flush of youth, of florid good looks and hearty manner. But now, as he came towards her, Peri realised, from the fumes of spirit on his breath, that he had been drinking and was not his usual self. She knew him to be a wealthy man with huge estates in Northumberland and an excellent head for business, but Peri had always privately thought him the perfect country squire, with his quiet, dark suits and his easy manners. She ran a critical eye over the magnificence of a puce coat, pink embroidered waistcoat and fawn breeches, and thought he looked uneasy in such finery with his red face and his wig slightly askew.

'Help me?' he said, slurring his words a little. 'Well, Martha, your mistress asked me to give you this fan. She di ... din't want his lordship to see, because one of the feathers snapped. He gave all the ladies a peacock fan, but only poor S'lina broke hers.'

'I'm sure it can be mended, sir,' Peri said, giving Mr Mapp an encouraging smile. 'But I'm not Martha, I'm Peri. It's my turn to undress Miss Selina tonight.'

He swayed forward a little and caught her shoulder as if for support.

'A tash ... task I envy you,' he said with immense solemnity. 'But in three nights' time, it will be I who undresh ... undresses your mistress!'

Peri giggled. 'Yes, I suppose ...'

'In three nights' time I shall be a married man,' Mr Mapp said mournfully. He caught hold of Peri's other shoulder and bent forwards, peering with owl-ish seriousness into the small face which seemed to be wavering before him. He brightened suddenly, a smile spreading across his flushed countenance. 'You're the slave, eh? When I'm a m-married man, you'll be *my* shla ... slave, won't you?'

'Yes, sir,' Peri agreed. It had not occurred to her, but she found she did not at all like the thought of being Mr Mapp's property.

'My slave!' His eyes glittered, scarcely a foot away from her own, and Peri began to feel very uncomfortable.

'Yes, sir,' she said again. 'Miss Selina will be here soon, I'll see that the fan is mended. And now I think you must go away.'

'Go away? Don't you find me attra ... attra ... handsome?' he said thickly. Before she could answer, he had lurched forward, pulling her into a hot and sweaty embrace. Peri struggled, Mr Mapp, laughing breathlessly, pushed against her, and they fell heavily on to the bed.

After that, everything became confused. Mr Mapp was half on top of her, calling her his 'dearesht Shelina' and pawing the bodice of her gown while Peri, trying to remove his hands, trying to dodge his brandy-laden breath, could only pray that she would be rescued.

The door opened at that point and Selina entered, saying over her shoulder, 'Do come and look at the fan, Pamela. The stick caught in the door-jamb and snapped right in ...' She stopped abruptly, staring at the scene of apparent debauchery taking place upon her bed. 'Dear God, Tufton! What on *earth* ...?'

'It's that little trollop,' Pamela said coldly, pushing past her friend. 'She's trying to seduce poor Mr Mapp just because he's in his cups.'

Mr Mapp, hearing voices behind him, lumbered to his feet and stood for a moment, swaying and blinking, before saying suddenly, 'Aaah, God, I'm going to be ill!' He stumbled across to the washstand and proceeded to vomit noisily into the big china bowl.

'I couldn't stop him, Miss Selina,' Peri said, sitting up with her gown off one shoulder and her hair tumbled down. 'He's had an awful lot to drink!'

'Even a drunken man needs some encouragement

to seduce a slave in her mistress's bedchamber,'
Pamela said spitefully.

Peri flushed. 'Mr Mapp needed none,' she protested hotly. 'Miss Selina, I think we ought to get
help for him.' She pointed at the unfortunate Mr
Mapp, still hanging over the china bowl and groan-
ing on an increasingly mournful note.

Help, however, was close at hand.

'What's to do? Selina, Mamma said your fan was
broken, and . . . Good God, what's Mapp doing?'

Standing in the doorway, an expression of considerable surprise on his face, Lord O'Neill looked
interrogatively at the three females.

'He came to return Selina's fan to her room, and
found that little trollop lying in wait for him.'

For the first time, the glance which his lordship
turned upon Miss Courtney was cold. 'What do you
mean, Pamela? Are you referring to Selina's maid?'

If Miss Courtney was taken aback by the chill in
his lordship's tone, she hid it well, taking his arm
and murmuring into his ear, 'Selina's had a nasty
shock, Crispin. When we came in Mr Mapp and
the slave were rolling on the bed, and he'd got her
gown half off. You would not distress your sister
by allowing her to think that Tufton tried to
seduce the girl?'

'Oh yes I would!' his lordship said frankly. 'I'll not
see the child suffer through no fault of her own. And
I'm very sure a little creature like Peri could scarcely
force Mapp to roll her on to the bed, even if she
wanted him to do so!'

'No?'

'No, Pamela,' Lord O'Neill said firmly. 'I dare say you meant it for the best, but I won't have it. One does not blame a servant when the master is at fault. Now you'd best go to your own room, there's nothing you can do here.'

While this low-voiced conversation was taking place, Selina and Peri were trying to bring comfort to the much afflicted Mr Mapp. As soon as his attentions to the bowl seemed at an end, Selina led him gently to a chair by the fire, and when he sank into it, she proceeded to bathe his face with her flannel, dipping it into the ewer of water which Peri carried across and stood by the chair.

'There, my dear, there! Shall I take your wig off? Do you feel a little better?'

Peri hovered watchfully, the empty milk pan in her hand, and his lordship suppressed a grin at the thought that if Tufton were to be ill again, the milk pan could scarcely stem the flood! However, Mr Mapp, leaning back in the chair and passing a trembling hand across his greenish countenance, seemed to be in control of himself for the moment.

'Look, he'd be best in bed,' Lord O'Neill said bluntly. 'Tufton, old fellow, can you walk?'

'Walk?' Tufton opened bloodshot eyes and winced in the firelight. 'I'll try.'

'Right. Peri, you get one side of him and I'll take the other. Between us we should get him to his room. Selina, you ring for a housemaid to clear up here. I'll send Peri back to help once he's in his room, and when I've dealt with the task of getting him into bed, I'll come back. Wait for me, there's a good girl.'

'Very well,' Selina said. She still looked a trifle dazed. 'Don't be long.'

Within five minutes Peri was back, saying anxiously, 'Indeed, Miss Selina, it was not my fault! He thought I was you, and kept calling me Selina. But I'm very sorry it happened.'

'So am I,' Selina answered ruefully. 'And by tomorrow I'm sure Mr Mapp will feel the same, if he does not already. Now don't you worry, for I'm sure it was not your fault. Will you have time to help me to change and tidy myself before my brother returns?'

'I think so,' Peri said with a little chuckle. 'When I left them, his lordship and Mr Mapp's valet were holding Mr Mapp's head over another basin, and the valet was saying that his master's best embroidered waistcoat was quite ruined. And his lordship said he'd help the valet to get Mr Mapp into bed when the vomiting was finished.'

'Oh, poor Tufton,' Selina said feelingly. 'Very well then, I'll change into my nightgown.'

Working quickly, Peri had her mistress neatly nightgowned, her hair brushed free from powder and her face washed clean, by the time his lordship returned. A housemaid had tidied the wash-stand and had just delivered a clean china bowl when Lord O'Neill tapped and entered.

'That's better,' he said with relief, looking from the tidy room to his sister's once more placid countenance. 'Off with you, Peri, my sister and I want a quiet word before she goes to bed.'

Peri went obediently through into the dressing-room and closed the intervening door, then dropped to her knees beside it and proceeded to listen intently.

'It *was* Tufton's doing, you know, Selina. I know Pamela only said what she did to spare your feelings, but Tufton himself admits it. I dare say you didn't realise he was in his cups, but he's all remorse now, I assure you.'

'I've no doubt,' Selina said dryly. 'What am I to do, Cris? I don't want to be unkind, but I won't take Peri to London with me! I wouldn't have a moment's peace after this, thinking ...'

'Look, once he's married to you, there will be no need for Tufton to chase a slave! It's just that his natural urges ... well, the wedding's so close, and ...'

His lordship lost himself in sentences which became increasingly disjointed as he spoke.

'No! I *won't* take her to Paris with us, and I won't have her in London! You know how easy-going I am, but for once I'm putting my foot down. You didn't buy Peri for me in the first place, you bought her ...' There was a pause, and then Selina continued in a calmer tone, 'You bought her on impulse. I won't take her to London with me, knowing that Tufton will be ogling her all the time and perhaps wishing to seduce her. You've said yourself she's a fetching little piece, and I won't have her fetching my husband!'

'It doesn't matter, she can stay here, and no doubt Mamma will train her for Eleanor. After all, I'd no intention of giving you a burden!' His lordship had been speaking stiffly, but suddenly his voice softened. 'I say, old girl, don't cry! Upon my honour, Tufton meant nothing by it. Damme, he was in his cups, no more responsible for his actions than a babe in arms! And don't worry about Peri; I'll take care of her, with Mamma's assistance.'

'If ... if you're sure it will be all right?' Peri's listening ears heard her mistress gulp, and then regain control over her wobbly voice. 'You see, Cris, I love Tufton! I know he's a good match and very rich and everyone in London envied me, but ... it isn't his money, or estates, or anything. He's nowhere near so handsome as you or Jerome, he isn't tall, or young or anything. But I love him, and I couldn't bear to think he didn't love me!'

'Of course he loves you!' His lordship employed his most bracing tone. 'And now dry your eyes and hop into bed. By morning you'll see the whole thing in perspective. Though it's a confounded nuisance that Pamela should have seen what went on. D'you think she'll spread it around?'

'Not if you ask her to say nothing. She's waiting for you to offer for her, you know.'

'D'you think so?' His lordship sounded abstracted, to Peri's glee. 'Well, she'll have to wait until after the wedding, at any rate.'

'Cris, are you sure you want to marry her? I know she's rich, and very beautiful, but ...'

'Damme, of course I do!' His lordship sounded quite shocked. 'Have I not said so any time these twelve months? The prettiest girl in England, and the sweetest. But she understands that I must do my duty by my family first.'

'Yes, of course. Goodnight then, brother.'

'Goodnight, Selina.'

Peri crouched for a moment longer by the door, then, as she heard the unmistakable sounds of his lordship's footsteps retreating down the corridor and Selina's bed creaking as she climbed into it, she turned and got into her own pallet. She lay down, the words she had overheard going round and round in her head. So he *was* going to marry that horrible Miss Courtney! And she herself was to stay here, instead of going away with Selina. She would be with his lordship! That fact alone was blissful enough to make the possibility of his marrying Miss Courtney seem less terrible.

For a moment longer she fought sleep, considering what she had heard. She would be trained as lady's maid by the Dowager Lady O'Neill, so that later she might wait upon Miss Eleanor. That would be nice, she thought drowsily. Eleanor was a lively young creature with a deal of bounce and humour. And of course, his lordship had not even offered for Miss Courtney yet! Taking one thing with another it was pointless to worry about something which, if she was clever, might never happen. She wondered how Miss Courtney would feel about, say, beetles? Suppose there was to be a plague of beetles, in her bed-chamber? Or rats? Poisonous snakes would be best, of course, but she had no idea whether such creatures were readily available in England. Beetles were frequently to be seen in the kitchen and pantries late at night, and rats abounded in the outbuildings.

She had not abandoned her idea of administering

a dose of poison, but from her veiled attempts to find out about such things in the servants' hall, it seemed as though poisons might be difficult to lay one's hands on here, and though the servants had heard of wise women, they did not seem to place much faith in their powers, save for the curing of warts and certain diseases in cattle. Indeed, when she had asked casually whether the wise women ever laid a wasting disease on anyone's farm stock, Albert, the footman, had said that anyone trying that trick would speedily find themselves labelled 'witch'.

'And then she wouldn't last long,' he had added darkly.

So Peri, lying snugly in bed, concluded that whatever she did to Miss Courtney would have to be done by herself alone. Not that that worried her!

I'll find a way, she was saying to herself as she drifted off to sleep.

CHAPTER
FIVE

THE wedding had gone off very well. Selina, her golden tresses brushed and curled by Peri until they shone, wore a gown of white figured satin and carried a bouquet of white lilies. The only colour was in her hair, the blue of her eyes and the glorious wild rose in her cheeks and lips, for she was very happy, and after the ceremony she clung to Tufton's arm, chattering away to him, while he smiled down at her with a pride and fondness which brought a lump to more than one throat.

When the wedding breakfast was over the bride and groom drove off in one coach, followed by another containing all their luggage and Martha, while Eleanor waved and Lady O'Neill wept a little, and was hugged by her son and comforted by her nephew.

'Indeed, ma'am, you should rejoice in their happiness,' Jerome told his aunt. 'A better man than Tufton Mapp you'd go a long way to find. And Selina is so happy!'

To his cousin, however, Jerome was more forthright. 'God knows I wouldn't care to be shut away in Northumberland for six months of the year, but no doubt Selina will endure it happily, because Tufton will be with her. Now, old fellow, tell me what your plans are! There's dancing and feasting for the rest of the day, eh? Parties for the servants and for the villagers, I suppose. How long will it be before you go to London for the rest of the Season?'

'Oh, a couple of weeks, I dare say,' Lord O'Neill said airily. 'But you're at liberty to leave when you wish!'

Jerome smiled, at his most saturnine. 'Leave when I wish? My dear coz, while the delightful Miss Courtney remains beneath your roof, nothing would drag me away.'

'Oh! Well, since Mamma is acting as Pamela's chaperon, she will stay here until we go to London.'

If he hoped to discompose his cousin, his lordship was doomed to disappointment. 'Then so shall I,' Jerome assured him earnestly. 'So shall I!'

Peri meanwhile, bereft of her friend Martha and of her mistress, took herself into the Dowager's room in a frame of mind both doleful and doubtful. How would she please a lady so elderly? For Lady O'Neill was quite forty-five! However, her ladyship's dry common sense, and a motherliness which warmed Peri's young heart, soon won her affection. She listened patiently as the Dowager outlined her duties, adding that her own lady's maid, Moorfield, would be glad to advise her.

'You may assist Moorfield, and you'll learn a lot that way. It would, I think, be beneficial to both you and Miss Eleanor if you were to go to her room night and morning and help her into and out of her clothes. You would both learn a good deal, I dare say. Then, if his lordship decides to leave you with Eleanor when we go to London presently, you will already be of some use to her.'

Peri curtsied as she had been taught, but said, 'Leave me behind? Oh, no! I was sure I'd go to London!'

The Dowager smiled, but made no comment, and presently Peri found herself free for a few moments. She made her way at once along the corridors to his lordship's room and entered, after only the most cursory tap on the door.

'Sir! Why may I not go to London with you?'

Lord O'Neill, quietly sitting in a chair by the window and smoking a small cigar, jumped and swore.

'Peri! What on earth do you mean, bursting in on me like that? You shouldn't come to my bed-chamber!'

Peri sniffed disdainfully, then crossed the room, to lean against his chair arm, looking down at him. 'How else can I talk to you?' she enquired reasonably. 'I never see you. And I *do* want to go to London when you go!'

He was amused and stood up, looking down into her enquiring face. 'So you shall, if it means so much to you! And I'll tell you what—there is a fair on in Liverpool. You've never been to a fair, I'll warrant. If I have time, I'll arrange for the servants to go down there one afternoon, in a farm cart. You'd enjoy it prodigiously.'

He could not help a fleeting regret that he would not see her pleasure. But at the same moment the thought of taking Pamela to the fair struck him. How she would enjoy the sideshows, the entertainments, the theatrical booth! He imagined himself guiding her through the wonders, watching her wide-eyed enjoyment of such frivolities as a dancing bear, the fattest woman in England, the fire-swallower. Sophisticated as Pamela was, he had little doubt that she had never attended a fair, for her father would certainly not have allowed her to frequent such a low place.

'What is a fair?' Peri asked doubtfully. 'But it doesn't matter. Do you mean that I may go to London? Oh, you are so good to me!'

Before he could exclaim or object—if, indeed, he had any intention of doing either—she had jumped up, flung her arms round his neck, kissed his chin, and was on her way back to the door.

'Hey, wait a minute,' he called, but she only turned to give him a dimpling smile before disappearing down the long corridor in the direction of his mother's room.

She left his lordship stroking his chin thoughtfully, still feeling the impression of her young body against his own, the warmth of her arms round his neck.

After considerable manoeuvring, Lord O'Neill had at last managed to get Miss Courtney to himself. It was after dinner that night, and they strolled once more in the yew walk, though Lord O'Neill, after their previous experience here, kept a wary lookout as they passed each shadowy tree.

'There's a fair on in the city,' he said at last, when they had gained the rustic bench. 'You've never been, I suppose?' Then, as Pamela shook her head, 'Well, I'd like to take you there tomorrow night. You could be masked, of course, and cloaked. It's great fun, with all sorts of stalls and booths, and there are fireworks at midnight, and dancing. What do you say?'

'Tomorrow night? Oh, I don't think so, Crispin.' Miss Courtney's small nose wrinkled with distaste. 'It will be alive with Cits and yokels.'

'Well, yes, but you'll be masked,' his lordship persisted. 'Do say you'll come, Pamela.'

'I'll think about it,' the beauty said slowly. And after a little desultory talk of the wedding, and the London Season at present getting into its swing, they returned to the house.

By the following evening, the whole household had learned of the fair, and the servants were all eager to go. However, despite his promise, Lord O'Neill had completely forgotten to arrange for a farm cart to take them into the city. Albert suggested to Peri that he and she might slip away, but Albert had taken quite a fancy to Peri, and she had already realised that his attentions could all too easily become embarrassing, so she declined the treat.

However, should a cart be made available so that all might go, she was only too eager to taste the delights of the fair. She, Polly and Sue, two of the housemaids, were hanging about the hall, hoping to hear that a cart would be calling for them, when Peri was summoned to his lordship's study.

'Yes, sir?' she said, slipping into the room, her small face eager.

'Peri, would you run down to the lodge for me and ask Mrs Pershore if she could make up the hot lemon cure which she used to give Selina for her headaches? Pam ... Miss Courtney has a bad head, and I thought it might ease her.'

'Of course,' Peri said at once. She wished she might spill the lemon cure, or put something disgusting into it as she carried it back to the Hall, but that would never do, being directly traceable to herself.

'Good girl,' said his lordship approvingly. 'Now run, Peri, because I'd planned to take Miss Courtney to the fair, and if I can but cure her headache there may still be time to have some fun.'

'The fair?' Peri, who had been making her way out of the study, swung round. 'Ooh!' It was a gasp of longing. 'How I'd love to go!'

'I'll arrange for the servants to go tomorrow,' his lordship said, belatedly remembering his promise. 'Now off with you. And run!'

Run Peri did, for to be tardy and cause his lordship pain was not to be thought of. But when she arrived back, panting, with the cure neatly bottled and stoppered, his lordship told her to take it straight to Miss Courtney, and to give her the verbal instructions in its use which Mrs Pershore had given her.

However, when she reached Miss Courtney's room, she found her way barred. Miss Courtney's maid, a brusque, thin-lipped Scotswoman called Chapman, answered the door. The room seemed to be in darkness and Chapman, her mouth tightening instinctively at the sight of Peri's slight figure, said impatiently, 'Yes?'

'His lordship's sent a cure for Miss Courtney, which his nurse made up for him,' Peri explained, handing over the bottle. 'If I may see Miss Courtney I'll explain how the dose is to be taken, and ...'

She was speaking to a closed door.

Making her way downstairs to the study, she explained she had been unable to gain admittance to the sufferer's chamber, nor had she been allowed to explain how the dose should be taken.

'Oh, Chapman, that sour old maid,' his lordship muttered. He sprang to his feet. 'I'll go up myself. You wait here.'

But alas, even his lordship's personal representations cut no ice with the formidable Chapman.

'Miss Courtney's no' herself,' she said stiffly. 'Aye, I'll see she teks the med'cine, but she'll no' go out the night, and she'll no' see anyone.'

Lord O'Neill, returning to Peri waiting in his study, said sulkily, 'I dare say there's nothing the matter with Pamela at all, save that she dislikes the company of Cits and yokels! I'm sure she seemed well enough at dinner, laughing and joking with Jerome and telling me that snuff-taking was a more elegant habit than smoking cigars.' He turned to Peri, his face suddenly lighting into mischief. 'I'll tell you what, brat, you and I shall go! What do you say? You'll have a wonderful time!'

It was no sooner said than accomplished. In a whirl of enjoyment Peri found herself wrapped in a dark cloak, with a handkerchief tied round her curls to save them from being blown about her face in his lordship's coach. And then they were off, heading for the city, with his lordship driving, Peri tucked in close beside him and Simkins, his groom, hanging on behind.

During her ride to the Hall in the coach, Peri had been able to see only a restricted view of the countryside but now, perched up by his lordship on the box, she realised that the road wound along the shore, with only the sandhills and the marram grass between it and the sea on the right-hand side.

'Oh, the sea! When my parents were alive we lived almost on the shore. It was lovely to play on the beach, with the white sand, and the sea so warm and blue.' She sighed, glancing up at him. 'I'd like to walk on the beach one day.'

'What?' his lordship said, raising his voice against the wind. 'Oh, the beach! Yes, it can be a pleasant walk. But wait till you see the fair! What do you think of my driving? I can drive to an inch, so don't be afraid!'

He feathered a corner in fine style, but his leader slipped a trifle on the loose sand which was constantly blown across the road and, prudently, he slackened the pace.

'It's exciting,' Peri said enthusiastically. 'Go faster, milord!'

He laughed, glancing down into the vivid little face so near his shoulder. 'You mean it, don't you? But I dare not, not here! It's the sand, you see; it makes the corners damned dangerous. One day

I'll take you from London to Brighton, and *then* we'll spring 'em!'

She sighed, snuggling closer to him, and he realised suddenly that one did not promise a slave that one would drive her along the most fashionable thirty miles in England in an open carriage! But never mind, this evening was hers. Pamela could not help having a headache, of course, though he had a shrewd suspicion that it came largely from a distaste for common amusements.

All too soon, it seemed to Peri, they arrived at the piece of ground where the fair was being held. Lord O'Neill reined in his horses, the groom ran to their heads, and his lordship jumped lightly down to the ground and held up his arms to Peri.

She jumped unhesitatingly, and for a few seconds he held her warm little body close, feeling the thumping of her heart against his own, before he stood her down.

'There!' He turned to the groom. 'Stable the horses at the Wheatsheaf, Simkins. When we've had a look round the fair we'll get some supper in the coffee-room and send a message out to the stables for the carriage.'

Simkins touched his hat and led the equipage away, and Lord O'Neill looked down at his young companion with a grin. 'And now, young lady, for the fair!'

For the next couple of hours it would have been difficult to say who enjoyed themselves the most. They visited the fattest lady in England, and saw her dance a measure with the thinnest man. They tried

their luck at various side-shows, and his lordship
won a bunch of rainbow-coloured ribbons and tied
the scarlet ones then and there into Peri's dark curls.
They squeezed into a theatrical booth and watched
an exciting—and bloodthirsty—performance of a
play which seemed to consist largely of persons
fighting, and stabbing other persons, with a great
shedding of artificial blood over both stage, and, in
one instance, the front row of the audience so that
Peri, ducking back with a squeal, bumped heads
with his lordship and became almost helpless with
laughter.

Presently, coming out of the theatrical booth, it
seemed natural for Lord O'Neill to put his arm about
Peri's waist, the easier to guide her through the
crowd. It seemed even more natural to Peri that she
should cuddle close to her idol.

Their next visit was to the fire-eater's booth, and
they watched goggle-eyed as the fire-eater proceeded
to consume a meal of red-hot coals, flaming brimstone, quantities of boiling pitch and other unusual
comestibles. Presently, his barker announced that
Mr Powell would fill his mouth with red-hot coals
and broil a slice of beef on his tongue, provided the
silver-collection made it worth his while. Lord
O'Neill, having seen enough, would have walked
away at that point had not Peri, fairly dancing with
excitement, clutched him so hard and entreated his
generosity so earnestly that he tossed half a guinea
into the collecting plate.

Such largesse enabled Mr Powell not only to broil
the slice of beef to everyone's satisfaction, but to melt

a quantity of beeswax, sealing wax, brimstone, alum
and lead over a chafing dish of live coals, and having
reduced his entire audience to breathless anticipation by watching the simmering of this deadly-
seeming brew, he proceeded to eat it with a spoon,
referring to it as 'my nice, 'ot soup', a finale which
had everyone gasping.

Still entwined, Lord O'Neill and Peri left the fire-
eater's booth and wandered off in search of the
Learned Pig, encountering on the way a seller of
gilded gingerbread, and an urchin offering lumps
of 'jaw-breaker', a particularly hard and sticky
toffee.

Naturally, to one intent upon tasting all the
pleasures of the fair, toffee and gingerbread could not
go unpurchased; Peri, one cheek bulging with toffee,
one hand clutching a slab of gloriously sticky gingerbread, looked so pretty and happy that Lord O'Neill
quite forgot that he was keeping company with a
slave, and felt proud of his Peri.

'The dancing bear! Oh, do let us see,' pleaded Peri
presently. Not at all averse, Lord O'Neill shouldered
his way to the front of the crowd, propelling his
charge before him, until they had a good view of the
shaggy, muzzled beast with its twinkling humorous
eyes, turning and stamping in its dance to the music
of a thin and reedy pipe.

'I wish I could give the bear some gingerbread,'
Peri said presently. 'Doesn't he dance nicely?'

'Well,' Lord O'Neill was beginning guardedly, for
he thought the bear's long claws looked dangerous,
when Peri grabbed his arm.

'Sir! Your cousin Jerome—Mr Harcourt, I mean—is over there. With a lady!'

'What? Damme, so he is! Thought he'd gone off to visit our Aunt Nell out at Wavertree,' his lordship said, but without much interest. 'With a lady, did you say? That was quick work! But I can't see her.'

He glanced towards where his cousin had been, but a movement of the crowd now hid both Jerome and his companion, and presently Lord O'Neill reminded his fair charge that they had not yet found the tent where ale, beer and even ratafia was on sale, for despite his undoubted enjoyment of the entertainment, an enjoyment doubled by Peri's innocent delight in everything her eyes alighted on, his lordship was becoming very dry.

They pushed their way out of the good-humoured crowd again and found their way to the refreshment tent, where Lord O'Neill paid far too much for a glass of beer for himself and a lemonade for his flushed, ecstatic companion.

It was whilst they were seated on some strawbales, thoughtfully provided by the management, and drinking, that Peri nudged his lordship once more.

'Here's Mr Harcourt and his friend,' she hissed.

'Aye, so they are,' murmured Lord O'Neill. 'A quick worker, my cousin Jerome, though his wench is a bit pale and skinny for my liking.' He squeezed Peri. 'I like a cuddly little creature like you,' he said teasingly. 'You're slender in all the right places, and ...'

He paused, staring at Jerome's companion and

then, with a crashing oath, he was on his feet, pulling Peri up after him, trying to force his way through the crowd towards the other couple.

'Sir! What's the matter?' Peri squeaked. She had recognised that pale gold hair the moment she set eyes on it, but she was enjoying herself too much to want the evening to end disastrously.

'That's *Pamela*,' Lord O'Neill said between clenched teeth. 'The lying jade! She's even now supposed to be laid on her bed with the headache! As for Jerome, I'll tear him limb from limb, I'll . . .'

'It's no use, they've gone out of the tent. We'll never find them in this crowd,' Peri said miserably.

'We'll have a damned good try,' Lord O'Neill said grimly. He pushed his way out of the tent, towing the reluctant Peri behind him.

However, only a very few moments were sufficient to confirm Peri's remarks. In that crowd, only luck would bring them up with their quarry.

'And Jerome saw me, damn his eyes,' his lordship said, drawing Peri to a halt and ruefully rubbing his forehead. At her woebegone expression, however, he burst out laughing. 'I'm a fool! It couldn't have been Pamela, she's far too honourable to play me such a trick. Come on, little one, let's find the Learned Pig.'

They found the Learned Pig and saw him count up to ten, find a hidden handkerchief, and shake his head when he meant no. After this display of wisdom they felt in need of amusement once more, so visited a puppet show which had Peri talking of magic, and the little people. Then they ate sausages on sticks and potatoes baked in their jackets over a charcoal burner. Then, still entwined, they watched a fire-work display which had Peri gasping and squeaking and, finally, his lordship led his charge back to the Wheatsheaf.

'I say, what a little gipsy you look,' he said, as they stood before the inn. In the light streaming from the windows he examined the small face turned anxiously up to his. 'Here, I'd better tidy you up a bit or they'll not let me take you into the coffee-room.'

He produced a comb from the recesses of his coat and dragged it ruthlessly through the dark, tangled curls, then licked his handkerchief and cleaned off the smears of toffee, gingerbread and charred potato which decorated his companion's mouth.

At last he held her at arm's length, admiring his handiwork. 'There! You look quite . . .' his voice died away. The small, heart-shaped face tilted up to his, the big eyes shining with adoration, the soft mouth trembling into a smile in anticipation of his praise. He continued to stare at her. She was beautiful! He felt his heart move, a strange, aching tug, and he knew he wanted to take her in his arms, to kiss that kissable mouth, feel her close to him, where she belonged.

Then a hand caught at his shoulder.

'Hello, Cris! What are you doing here with Peri? I thought she was only a child!' It was Jerome, his dark face sarcastic, a grin lurking.

Self-consciously, his lordship's hands, which were still grasping Peri's shoulders, dropped to his sides. 'Jerome! Who were you with?' he said sharply.

'Who *was* I with? I still am, only she's gone into the

inn to tidy herself up. Lucy, the barmaid from the Feathers. Why, do you know her?' He chuckled. 'A pretty, knowing little wench! I doubt I'll be back at Brownlow Hall tonight!'

Some of the stiffness left his cousin's attitude. 'Oh! A barmaid, eh? What does she look like?'

Jerome's dark glance rested on Peri for a moment. What he read in her eyes seemed to please him, for he smiled slightly, then looked back at Lord O'Neill. 'What? Oh, what does she look like? Well, she's not as pretty as Peri here! She's a yeller-head, with blue eyes and a nice shape. Why? Do you fancy your chances with her? I'll exchange her for Peri any day.'

Peri shrank closer to Lord O'Neill, who said shortly, 'I think not. And now we'll say goodnight, coz. I'm going to get Peri some supper, and then take her home.'

Jerome shrugged. 'As you please. But the night's young. We could have some fun with the two girls, and ...'

'Goodnight, Jerome.'

Lord O'Neill swung abruptly away, leading Peri into the coffee-room. 'Come and have some hot chocolate,' he said gruffly. 'You'll like that.'

Peri, totally unaware that his lordship had come within ames-ace of forgetting himself towards her, chattered on happily as she drank hot chocolate and devoured ham sandwiches. She noticed that he seemed a little quieter than usual, and that his eyes rested on her sometimes with a strange expression in their depths, but thought it merely remorse over his unfounded suspicions of Pamela, aggravated, perhaps, by tiredness.

'I've had the most wonderful evening of my life,' she said, when he had paid their reckoning and he was handing her back into the carriage.

He settled down in his seat and squeezed her shoulders. 'Yes, it's been a grand evening,' he agreed. 'Good thing it's a fine night! Not that I intend to drive fast.'

And indeed, he drove back very slowly, for within five minutes of getting into the vehicle, Peri had fallen fast asleep, her head pillowed comfortably upon his caped, driving-coated shoulder.

She did not stir until they reached the stableyard, when he woke her gently and lifted her down to stand, swaying, on the cobblestones, saying dreamily, 'A beautiful, beautiful evening. *Thank* you, milord.'

He put his arm round her and led her into the house. Everywhere was quiet, and he walked her slowly up the stairs. On the top landing he stopped.

'Where do you sleep now that Selina's gone? In Lady O'Neill's dressing-room?'

'No, in the attics. I have a little room up there.'

He hesitated. Damme, but she was a darling! Then, somewhere along the corridor, a door opened and closed softly. Quickly, his lordship pulled Peri into the darkened foot of the attic stairs. Miss Chapman, her face set in its usual lines of sourness, came past, a candle in one hand, Mrs Pershore's bottle of headache cure in the other. It was, his lordship was pleased to see, half empty, proving to his fond mind that Pamela had been taking the stuff in her sickbed.

Lord O'Neill waited until Miss Chapman's bony back had disappeared down the stairs, then nudged Peri.

'Wake up, child! Up you go, and sleep well.'

He patted her shoulder, then propelled her firmly towards the attic stairs and watched as she stumbled up them, half-asleep still. At the top she glanced back, gave him a small, weary smile, and then turned into the first doorway on the right.

Lord O'Neill, making his way back to his own room, was horrified to find himself repeating, 'The first doorway on the right', as he began to undress, having dispensed with the services of his exhausted valet as soon as his coat had been peeled off.

'It's not as if I've the slightest intention of taking advantage of the child,' he muttered, undoing his stock and throwing it in the general direction of the dressing-table. He began to unbutton his shirt rapidly, eager for the warmth of his bed. As he climbed into it, he told himself firmly that tonight had been a pleasant interlude, all the pleasanter, perhaps, for having a touch of wickedness about it. After all, one did not take one's servants to the fair, nor drive one's carriage with a child-slave asleep on one's shoulder. Or not, at any rate, if one was gathering one's courage to propose marriage to the toast of the *Beau Monde*!

He turned on his side, heaving the blankets up over his shoulders. It had been a grand evening, though!

And alone in her cold little room, undoing her buttons and fastenings with tired, chilly fingers, Peri woke up thoroughly long before she managed to strip off her last garment. It *had* been Miss Courtney at the fair; she was certain. Not only had she instantly recognised that wheat-gold hair, but the small mouth which showed beneath the mask had held just such a sneer as that which Miss Courtney usually turned upon the lesser servants.

And she had been with Mr Harcourt, his lord-ship's own cousin. Peri, jumping brisky into bed, sat up for a moment staring at the moonlit square of window, a frown between her soft brows. Why had Miss Courtney pretended a headache? It was surely impossible that anyone could prefer Mr Harcourt's company to that of his lordship? Or was it? Peri was innocent, but not too innocent to realise that the very things which most repelled her about Mr Harcourt might be fascinating to a girl reared in great luxury, every want satisfied, every selfish wish indulged. And by the same token, that which attracted her most strongly to his lordship—his protectiveness, his kindness, his air of firm authority, might seem boring to a girl who had known nothing but indulgent protection from birth.

The cold air was goosefleshing her shoulders, so she snuggled beneath the covers. It had been a mar-vellous evening, she thought, as she sank fathoms deep into slumber. A most marvellous evening!

CHAPTER
SIX

DESPITE his boast, it appeared that Mr Harcourt had slept at Brownlow Hall after all, for Peri met him descending the stairs as she was running up them, carrying a jug of hot chocolate for the Dowager. She would have passed him with no more than a smile, but he barred her way by the simple expedient of stopping, one hand on each banister, and smiling down at her.

'Well, Peri? What did you think of the fair?'

'It was wonderful,' Peri said enthusiastically, forgetting that Mr Harcourt was still in her black books. 'Did you see the Learned Pig, sir? And the fire-eater!' She beamed at the recollection. 'Oh, when he baked the piece of beef! But perhaps you didn't see that, because he did it specially for us when his lordship paid him a half-guinea!'

Jerome laughed. 'Are you insinuating that I'm too mean to pay a fire-eater half a guinea? Well, you're out as it happens, for we didn't go into the fire-eater's booth at all.'

'It was worth it,' Peri said earnestly. She glanced at the jug in her hand and added, 'I mustn't stop here talking to you though, sir. This chocolate will get cold.'

'Chocolate, is it? It's a miracle it isn't spilled all

down the stairs the way you were running up when I stopped you!'

She raised surprised eyes to his face. 'I never spill things. I run steadily, you see.'

'I see. And what would Miss Courtney say if she knew his lordship had taken you to the fair instead of her?'

The clear eyes were puzzled. 'If, sir? But she knows already. She saw me herself.'

Jerome chuckled, one eyebrow quizzically raised. 'Indeed? I thought you'd recognised her, Peri. What does his lordship think now that he knows the truth?'

Peri frowned. 'But he does not. He believed you, naturally.'

'Naturally!' he mocked softly. 'And you did not disillusion him? I can scarcely believe it!'

Peri stared up at him, an arrested expression on her face. 'Well, you may safely do so, for it's true,' she said slowly. She was wondering why on earth she had not taken the opportunity of assuring Lord O'Neill that Miss Courtney was every bit as false as he had thought her.

Jerome, correctly reading her expression, murmured, 'Precisely! But it's never too late to mend. Why don't you tell him this morning?'

The puzzled look cleared and the candid gaze was turned on him again. 'He would be very hurt, sir. He would feel ... cheated. So I shan't say anything.'

She could not fail to see the expression of chagrin which flickered across his countenance, but at that moment Moorfield emerged into the upper hall and glanced down the stairs.

'Peri, is that Milady's chocolate?' she said sharply. 'Don't hold her up, please, Mr Jerome, with your chatter.'

Jerome immediately stood to one side, bowing and grinning. 'I stand corrected! I beg pardon, Peri.' And then, as Moorfield turned on her heel and Peri mounted the last half-dozen stairs he added, in a whisper, 'Tell his lordship! It will be best.'

Peri ignored him, proceeding straight into the Dowager's room and meekly accepting Moorfield's strictures on servants who dallied with known rakes. But all the while her mind was in a turmoil. *Why* had she not seized the opportunity of letting his lordship see what a lying jade Miss Courtney was? She must have been mad! And yet she knew she would not say that Miss Courtney had gone to the fair with Mr Harcourt; that Miss Courtney was a liar and had told her servant to lie as well.

A little dose of poison or a plague of snakes would hurt Miss Courtney. But to see Miss Courtney in her true light would have hurt Lord O'Neill, and that, Peri now knew, was something she could never do. Love, it seemed, was a very powerful thing. As she tidied up after Moorfield, dusting powder off the dressing-table, cleaning the grate, teasing her lady-ship's wig into soft curls, she wondered at her own foolishness. For surely it was foolish not to tell? What if he married Miss Courtney believing her to be an honest woman, and was made unhappier by finding out too late that she was not?

Yet somewhere within her was the conviction that his lordship was too wise to be taken in by Miss Courtney's wiles for long. He would see through the other girl without any help from his adoring slave. Comforted by this thought, Peri continued with her work, putting the thought of Miss Courtney right out of her mind. Soon she was singing snatches of a popular song that his lordship liked as she dusted and cleaned.

Miss Courtney would surely suffer for her sins, she thought as she worked. Retribution was nigh, especially if she could lay her hands on a viper or two! And then his lordship would never need to know that his company had been spurned for that of his worthless, rakish cousin!

Miss Courtney, meanwhile, being indifferent to the opinions of those she considered her inferiors, had no idea that Peri disliked her. But last night had provided a most salutary lesson. She had gone to the fair with Jerome because he intrigued her with his rakish indifference to propriety, and his air of being a dangerous companion. Lord O'Neill's invitation had been refused on the grounds that since she had every intention of marrying his lordship, she should not be seen by servants and commoners visiting the fair, for no one would doubt that she was Crispin's companion, be she never so well masked.

Although she had no intention of marrying Jerome, whom she knew to be a rake and a libertine, one who had already gamed and womanised his way through a considerable fortune, she did wish to add

him to her list of conquests. Had her mother been
alive, it was doubtful whether she would have got
nearer to Jerome than the opposite side of a ballroom. But her indulgent Papa, seeing that she was in
a fair way to capturing a most eligible *parti* in Lord
O'Neill, had agreed that she might spend a month at
Brownlow Hall before joining him at his London
house.

She had felt pleasantly wicked at the fair with
Jerome, until that moment in the refreshment tent,
when she had seen Crispin leap to his feet with an
oath, and had thought herself discovered. She had
panicked, insisting that Jerome take her home
instantly and then return himself, with any blonde
female he had been able to find. She had rushed back
to her room dry-mouthed with fear, telling herself
that if she escaped detection she would never act so
foolishly again. If she failed to retain her hold on
Lord O'Neill's affections, she knew that half the
mammas in the Polite World would be delighted.
His name, his acres and his huge fortune were
enough for most. Add to that his fair curls, bright
blue eyes and his considerable charm, to say nothing
of his height and figure, and it was small wonder that
Miss Courtney's heart sank at the recollection of her
own madness.

So she had gone, shaking, to bed, furious with
herself for her behaviour. And then, safe beneath the
blankets, she began to feel annoyed with him.
Unjustifiably, perhaps, yet that did not lessen her
indignation.

How dare Lord O'Neill take a slave to the fair in

her stead! There she was, lying on her bed of sick-
ness—or so he had supposed—and what had he
done? He had forgotten all about her and góne
a-pleasuring with Peri!

She had seen Peri's face quite clearly as they stood
opposite one another watching the dancing bear,
and had noted the upward, adoring glance which the
girl directed towards his lordship. *So it's like that, is it?*
she had thought spitefully. Now, she folded her lips
tightly, telling herself that no doubt Crispin had
taken her home and tumbled her, and would expect
to be welcomed back by herself with open arms.

The maddening thing was that she could not blaze
contemptuously at him, giving vent to jealous fury,
without admitting she had seen him there. Unless
she could persuade Jerome to pretend that he had
told her? It would be typical of Jerome to have
passed on such an interesting titbit, for she was
aware that there was rivalry between the two cousins
over herself.

She pondered the possibility of this for a moment.
She did not, of course, acknowledge that she was
jealous of Peri; such an emotion could not be aroused
by a slave! She wanted to revenge herself on Crispin
for the fright he had given her, but it might be best, in
the circumstances, to forget the entire episode.

On the morning after the fair, very early, she
opened her bedroom door and let Jerome in, as they
had arranged the previous evening. She knew this to
be wrong, even foolish, but she had to know whether
their plan had fooled Lord O'Neill.

As soon as Jerome slipped round the door, closing

it softly behind him, she could tell their deception had been successful.

'All went merry as a wedding bell,' he announced. 'I got back to the fair and befriended a pretty little blonde trollop, wrapped her in your cloak and mask and paraded her about. I quite disarmed Crispin's suspicions, I assure you.'

'Good,' Miss Courtney said, but there was a trace of annoyance in her tone and Jerome, with his considerable knowledge of the female mind, had no difficulty in recognising that Miss Courtney was jealous of her replacement.

'I knew you'd be pleased,' he said falsely. 'She played up well, bless her! I told Cris I'd be spending the night with her, to put him completely off the scent, and then drove back here at dawn.'

Miss Courtney found herself feeling even more vexed with Jerome's yellow-headed trollop than with Crispin and Peri. 'Good,' she said again. 'I'll see you at breakfast.'

She gestured towards the door, dismissively, but Jerome did not move.

'Miss Courtney! Pamela! I thought better of you. I've saved your reputation, spent a boring evening with a tavern-wench, suffered a damned cold night in my carriage trying to get a few hours' sleep, and what's my reward? A cold "good"!'

She smiled, glancing at him with more approval. So he had not spent the night with his tavern-wench, after all, nor enjoyed her company! And with no more encouragement than the smile, he swept her into his arms, moulding her soft, uncorseted body against him, kissing her with such passion that her heart raced, though she put up a token resistance.

At last he held her away, smiling mockingly down into her flushed face.

'There! That's the sort of thanks a man appreciates. See you at breakfast!'

And he was gone, striding down the corridor on stockinged feet, back towards his own room. He left Miss Courtney torn between delight in his rough embrace and annoyance with herself for almost enjoying it.

She would have been surprised and horrified had she known that as he entered his own room he was muttering, 'I suspected as much! She's a cold fish, the sort that would drive a man to drink and other women within a week of marriage. However, she's rich, and who am I to object if I'm driven to drink and other women?'

Chuckling, he crossed the room towards his dressing-table. He began to brush his hair, glancing at himself in the mirror as he did so. Other women reminded him of that interlude in the stable with the slave-girl. The recollection of her soft lips beneath his own, the feel of her young body against him, made his breathing quicken. Now there was a female who could rouse the old Adam in a man! If only he had not been in such hot pursuit of the rich Miss Courtney he would have gone to considerable pains to make Peri his. She had fought against his embrace with far more fervour than Miss Courtney had shown, but once again his experience of women stood him in good stead. She

might not like him, but she would like lovemaking,
he was sure of it. He sat still, the hairbrush idle in
his hand, and dreamed of Peri's submission until
the chiming of the grandfather clock in the hall
brought him back to reality.

He tied his hair back from his face, straightened
his stock and got to his feet, an idea forming in his
mind. He had been warned off by Crispin, which was
fair enough. But suppose Pamela decided to settle for
eligibility in the form of Lord O'Neill rather than
romance and passion in the form of himself? Then,
surely, it would be fair if he took the slave-girl, as a
consolation prize?

It would certainly ease the sting of losing Pamela's
thousands, he reflected as he made his way down to
breakfast.

The fourth actor in the fairground drama, if such it
could be called, woke that morning consumed by
feelings of guilt. His lordship had believed his
beloved Pamela capable of the ugliest and lowest sort
of deception, and had been proved wrong. What a
swine he was! And he had done something almost
worse, for he could not deny that the evening at the
fair with Peri had been one of almost unalloyed
enjoyment. Nor could he deny his fondness for the
child. He had promised to take her to London without a thought for the consequences, the explanations
which such an act would call for. His mamma had
made it plain that if he and Pamela reached an
'understanding', as she put it, then his first duty
would be to call upon Lord Courtney in Berkeley

Square and obtain his formal consent to their betrothal. And where would Peri fit in? Until he was married he could scarcely claim to need a lady's maid amongst his retinue of servants, yet if she undertook some subervient position he might never see her! He was also forced to admit that Miss Courtney would not welcome Peri as a lady's maid. She had the grim, sharp-tongued Chapman, and unpleasant though the woman undoubtedly was, her affection for Pamela was not in question, nor her ability as a lady's maid. Also, he reminded himself, Peri was to become Eleanor's property, once she was trained in her work.

So what should he do with Peri? He kept his mind resolutely turned from what he would *like* to do with her! She was only a child, trustful and dependent, and he was a man of honour. He bit back the word 'unfortunately', then grinned at himself. What a fool he was! He was in love with Pamela, beautiful, gentle Pamela; what he felt for Peri was ... was ... well, it was quite different. Once he and Pamela were married he would not even think twice about a little slave-girl, no matter how appealing. He would send her back to Liverpool to wait upon his sister Eleanor, and think of nothing but his beautiful wife.

Lord O'Neill turned over in bed and burrowed back into the cool cotton pillow. Within five minutes he was asleep once more. And dreaming of Peri.

After luncheon, Peri had been told she might take time off until dinner, so decided to visit Mrs Pershore. Despite her promise to go and see the old lady, she had been so busy learning her duties that it had been impossible to snatch an hour or so to go down to the lodge. But this afternoon seemed ideal. The Dowager was visiting friends; Miss Courtney, Miss Eleanor and his lordship had gone, by coach, into Liverpool to visit the mantua maker who was making the clothes which Eleanor would need when she visited her sister in London, later in the season. And as she passed through the stableyard she had heard Mr Harcourt's voice, raised and angry, shouting at his groom, so it seemed safe to assume that he was riding out somewhere.

Peri sang to herself as she hurried along the drive. She heard the clatter of hooves behind her in good time, despite her song, and stood to one side to let Mr Harcourt, mounted on a tall bay stallion, pass.

It seemed as though he had not noticed her, standing still against the background of trees, but then he reined in his horse, twisted in the saddle and said cheerfully, 'Hello, Peri, where are you going? Want a ride?' He patted the horse's crupper invitingly.

Mindful of the last time she had been alone with him, Peri said firmly, 'No, thank you, sir. I'm only going down to the lodge to visit Mrs Pershore.'

He looked down at her, opened his mouth, shut it again, and then said, 'Very well, I'll walk my horse as far as the lodge with you.'

'I'd rather you didn't,' Peri admitted. 'It has such huge feet! I don't want to be trod on.'

He hesitated, then raised a hand in farewell and allowed the horse to break into a trot. 'Very well, little one. Be good!'

Once he was out of sight Peri relaxed and began to quicken her pace. She must be back in time to assist Moorfield in setting out her ladyship's evening clothes, so the sooner she arrived at the lodge the longer she and Mrs Pershore would have to gossip. It was nice, she reflected, to have someone for a friend. Although the servants were kind—particularly the menservants—she missed Martha. For some reason they treated Peri cautiously, almost politely, which did not make for ease. Mrs Pershore, she knew, could be relied upon to behave with her usual tartness, and she looked forward, with lively anticipation, to telling the older woman all about the fair, and the comings and goings up at the Hall. She also intended to ask a great many questions, especially about vipers.

But as it happened, she did none of those things. She knocked and knocked, but there was no answer. Mrs Pershore, it seemed, was out.

Stepping back from the door, Peri scanned the lodge. There was smoke coming from the chimney, so the fire was still in. Walking round the corner of the building, she saw the kitchen window was standing wide. Mrs Pershore had not gone far, or for very long.

For a moment she hesitated by the back door. Would it be locked? But it opened easily under her hand and she slipped inside, crossed the kitchen and went into the parlour. Sure enough the fire was lit and the kettle, full, stood in the hearth, waiting to be put upon the hob.

'Mrs Pershore will be glad of a cup of tea when she

gets back,' Peri muttered to herself, lifting the heavy kettle on to the hob. Then she went into the kitchen, helped herself to a piece of lump sugar, and returned to the parlour, to sit down by the fire and watch the kettle begin to hiss.

She had barely finished the sugar when she heard someone opening the back door. Hastily, so as not to startle her unwitting hostess, she called out, 'Mrs Pershore, it's Peri! I am come to visit you!'

The door opened, and the doorway was filled with the tall, dark-visaged figure of Jerome Harcourt. 'So you have, you pretty thing,' he said pleasantly. 'I quite forgot to tell you, when we met in the drive, that Mrs Pershore would be out. She visits Mrs Twiney, the keeper's wife, on a Wednesday.'

'Oh! Then I'll go home,' Peri said at once, moving towards the doorway. But Jerome made no attempt to stand aside.

'No, don't do that. Mrs Pershore will be back here in a few minutes. Didn't you hear Lady O'Neill say she was going to drop a parcel of sewing in at the lodge as she returns? Mrs Pershore will want to be here to receive it.'

'I dare say,' Peri said darkly, 'but I'm not waiting here with *you*, Mr Harcourt! Mrs Pershore would say it was not at all the thing. I wish you'd go!'

'How very impolite,' Jerome murmured. His eyes, glittering under the heavy lids, seemed half asleep but suddenly, almost before she had noticed him moving, he was standing only a foot away from her and his hands had shot out, grasping her by both shoulders, pulling her closer to him. 'Why so shy, Peri? I've told you Mrs Pershore won't be long. You're in no danger.'

'Danger? Of course not! But I dare say you mean to kiss me, which I don't like at all,' Peri answered stoutly. She tightened her mouth, staring up at him with an expression of mulish obstinacy on her small face.

'You don't like being kissed? You must be the only female I know who admits it,' Jerome said. Without effort he pulled her closer, so that she could feel the large buttons on his coat pressing into her small, firm breasts. 'Perhaps it's because you've not been kissed often enough.'

'I didn't say I disliked being kissed, I said I didn't like *you* kissing me,' Peri said frankly. 'Let me go if you please, sir.'

'But I don't please. I must teach you to like my kisses,' Jerome said. His smile was closer now as he bent his head towards her and Peri twisted in his grasp and brought her hands up, slapping his face as hard as she could first with her left hand, then her right.

'So the kitten has claws?' He was laughing, his breathing coming hard, but Peri knew, with a stab of fear, that he was annoyed. She found her arms imprisoned, felt her body crushed against him and then, slowly, leisurely almost, he began kissing her. She felt his lips against her throat, moving over the soft skin, taking his time, knowing she was pinioned too tightly to fight, that to scream would have been useless in this quiet spot.

But Peri was wilder than he knew, and more frightened. His lips aroused, not excitement, but the most frantic fear. She saw in her mind's eye the sailors on the *Tempest*, holding down the manacled, defenceless slave-women, before raping them. Jerome thought her innocent; but she knew, better than any of the fancy women he had kept, better than his married mistresses, better than Jerome himself, what animals men could become when lust drove them. As his lips travelled softly to the curve of her jawline he could feel the frantic, fluttering pulsebeats, and flattered himself that despite her words, she was beginning to be excited by his kisses. And then she turned her head sharply sideways, and her teeth sank into his cheek.

It was no kittenish nip, no love-bite. It was the real thing, with the ferocity and strength of a terrified young animal behind it.

Jerome cursed, on a shout of pain, and staggered back, loosing his hold on Peri just as a voice spoke from the doorway.

'A nice way to behave, Mr Jerome, just because you find my visitor alone.' Mrs Pershore, hatted, cloaked, comfortable, plodded into the room and set her basket down with a thud on the polished mahogany table. 'Dear me, that was heavy! Mrs Twiney sent me some honey, Peri-love. We'll have it to our tea. Run into the kitchen, there's a good girl, and cut some slices of bread for me. Then we'll toast 'em before the fire.'

Mrs Pershore's placid voice had the desired effect. Peri, the colour beginning to return to her face, scurried gladly out of the room and Mrs Pershore swung round on Jerome.

'Master Jerome, you should be ashamed! That poor child was wild with terror! Bit you, did she?' Regrettably, Mrs Pershore chuckled. 'That'll teach you!'

Jerome had been feeling his injured cheek cautiously; now he turned to Mrs Pershore, exhibiting his wound. 'Look at that! And damn it, I did nothing! A kiss! What's a kiss? You'd have thought I was trying ...'

'Yes,' Mrs Pershore said, 'I've no doubt, Mr Jerome, that she did think you was. You want to use a bit of imagination, sir. That poor little creature came from Africa, you know, with the blackbirders. It's a miracle she's as pretty and innocent as she is. We can't imagine the sights she must have seen, what she may have gone through herself.'

'Yes, but Pershy ... I mean to say ...' stammered Jerome, still fingering his cheek. 'Damn it, she's broken the skin! I'll have bruises there for a week!'

'You're lucky I came in when I did,' Mrs Pershore remarked placidly. 'Or I dare say she'd have drawn blood. A terrified creature fights with its full strength, sir, as you should know. You'd caught her hands, trapped her against you. Her only defence was to bite.'

'Well, if she'd said ... Hang it, what am I going to say when everyone asks what I've done to myself?' Jerome said furiously. 'I can't say Peri bit me!'

'Say you knocked yourself on a low branch,' Mrs

Pershore suggested. 'And now be off with you, Master Jerome. And on your way through the kitchen, just you apologise for treating the poor child like a dockside whore! Oh, you may shake your head at me, but you know full well that was no way to treat a gently-bred girl.'

Jerome, halfway to the door, turned and stared. 'Gently bred? Pershy, she's a slave!'

'Aye, so they tell me. But if you can't tell she's been properly brought up, gently bred, then you've no eyes in your head, sir. And now be off!'

Jerome entered the kitchen and looked across the room at Peri. She was cutting bread as she had been bidden but she looked up at his entrance and held his gaze, her own cool and steady.

'Peri, I'm sorry. But I swear I only wanted to kiss you. Upon my word, I'd not planned anything but a kiss. I knew Mrs Pershore would not be long, you see.'

Her eyes dropped and a flush warmed her cheeks. 'You frightened me very much, but I think I bit you hard, eh? I'm sorry too.'

He was touched, and held out his hand. 'Shall we be friends, then? Unless you want my kisses, I'll keep them to myself. Or risk getting bitten!'

'Very well.' She held out her own hand and he clasped it lightly then drew back and bowed.

'Goodbye for now, Peri. And thank you for accepting my apology so prettily.'

As soon as the back door closed behind him Peri flew back into the parlour, a toasting fork in one hand, a pile of sliced bread in the other. She impaled a slice of bread on the prongs and knelt before the fire.

'The kettle has boiled, Mrs Pershore. Will you make the tea?'

'Aye, in a moment.' Mrs Pershore looked hard into the small face, lit by the red glow from the fire. 'You all right now, Peri?'

'Oh, yes. Do you think Mr Jerome means that he won't kiss me again?'

Mrs Pershore hesitated, but honesty compelled her to say, 'He means it now, Peri, but I dare say he'll want to kiss you again. You're very kissable, you see, and Master Jerome's very susceptible.'

'What means susceptible?'

Mrs Pershore sighed and took the kettle into the kitchen. Having made the pot of tea and poured it into two mugs she returned, took her seat, and then began to butter the first round of toast while Peri speared a second slice.

'Susceptible means Mr Jerome likes pretty girls, my dear. Whilst his cheek is sore he'll be good, but he'll keep hoping you'll grow fonder of him. Keep him at arm's length, Peri.'

'How can I, when he grabs, and holds me so tight?' Peri said dolefully. 'I really don't like it, Mrs Pershore.'

'Of course you don't, dear,' Mrs Pershore said gently, recognising the understatement. 'I'll speak to her ladyship when she calls. That'll put a stop to his nonsense. And anyway, he'll be going to London soon and you won't be living under the same roof as him there. Mr Jerome's only a guest here.'

'Of course, I forgot that. Then I need only be careful for one more week.'

Mrs Pershore held out the first slice of toast, buttered and spread thickly with new honey, and Peri, sinking her teeth into it, was able to banish Jerome and her fears from her mind in the pleasure of this new taste.

And presently she returned to the Hall to prepare her ladyship's evening clothes, putting her troubles out of her mind.

CHAPTER
SEVEN

AFTER dinner, when Lord O'Neill and his cousin stood up to let the ladies leave the room, Lady O'Neill, passing her son's chair, told him quietly that when he had finished his port she would like to see him in her boudoir.

His lordship, who had hoped for a quiet half-hour with Pamela, agreed to go to his mother as soon as he could, and called for the decanter.

'Can't linger over the port this evening,' he said, pouring himself a brimming glass. 'My mother wants to see me. Don't you go stealing a march on me with Pamela though, Jer!'

'Oh!' Jerome remarked. His hand went up to his cheek, and noticing the marks for the first time, his cousin asked, 'What have you done to yourself?'

'Nothing much. A bite.'

'You've been scratching it,' his lordship said accusingly. 'That's why it's so swollen and inflamed. A horse-fly, was it?'

'Probably,' Jerome said, seizing the excuse gladly. 'I went riding this afternoon, over to Wavertree. I saw Aunt Nell and Aunt Felicity and they both sent you their regards.'

'I must go over myself before we leave for London.

They're nice old girls, and were kind to us when we were children.' Lord O'Neill drained his glass and stood up. 'If I'm to see Mamma and still have some evening left, I'd best go up now. And then, perhaps, we might attempt to teach Eleanor to make up a fourth at Loo, or Hazard.'

He left his cousin meditatively sipping port and, taking the stairs two at a time, went straight to his mother's boudoir. It looked cosy with the candles lit, the fire burning brightly and the curtains open to allow the low sunshine to pour into the room, for it was still only early evening. The Dowager had taken off her hoop and the stiff taffeta dress she had worn at dinner and was wrapped in a negligée. Moorfield had just finished plaiting her mistress's long hair into its bedtime plait and Peri was dusting the dressing-table and putting all to rights.

At her son's entry the Dowager smiled at him and said, 'Thank you, Peri, you may go down to the servants' hall now, and get some supper. And then come up to the dressing-room and finish your jobs there. I shan't want you again tonight. You might as well go too, Moorfield.'

Moorfield stumped out at once and Peri, after another cursory flick over the dressing-table with her duster, turned and glided past Lord O'Neill with lowered eyes, but as she drew level with him her glance flicked up to meet his and she gave him her sweet, mischievous smile. Then she was gone.

'Sit down, Crispin. Now we may be private. My dear, I want to talk to you about Peri.'

Lord O'Neill's eyebrows shot up. 'Indeed? Hasn't she pleased you?'

'Alas, she pleases not only me but everyone, including Jerome! I've sustained a lecture from Mrs Pershore and I've spoken to Peri herself. It seems that Rufus the gardener's boy tried to kiss her while she was cutting lilac for Eleanor's room, your valet pinched her bottom when she was carrying water upstairs three mornings ago, and Albert was becoming quite a nuisance with his attentions.' She paused, looking reflectively at her son's face. 'I say Albert *was* becoming a nuisance, because I believe he is a nuisance no longer. Peri assured me she tried politeness first.'

'First? Before what?'

'Before sticking a carving fork into the back of Albert's hand,' her ladyship said. 'He had to see the doctor, and now treats Peri with the greatest respect!'

'I'd da ... I'd like to know where his hand was, when he was stabbed,' his lordship said belligerently.

'According to Peri, it was travelling up her thigh, like a crab, under the shelter of the staff dining-table. One can scarcely blame her for reacting, though I felt that perhaps a little less force would have been just as effective. And now I come to Jerome.'

'I thought I'd put a stop to that,' his lordship said. 'I caught him in the stables, kissing the child, but I'm sure he won't do it again.'

Lady O'Neill sighed. 'Mrs Pershore returned home this afternoon, having been told by Twiney that Peri intended to visit the lodge, to find the girl defending herself against Jerome's persistent belief that she would, given time, learn to enjoy his kisses! Mrs Pershore was of the opinion that had she not entered the room when she did, considerable violence might have resulted. Peri bit Jerome, and your cousin was mightily annoyed.'

Lord O'Neill leapt to his feet. 'He dared ... after what I said to him, he *dared* ... By God, I'll not have him under my roof if he can't control his lusts! There are women enough in the 'Pool, God knows, if he needs ... wants ...' He stopped, suddenly remembering that it was to his mother that he spoke.

'I know, I know,' Lady O'Neill said soothingly. 'You must remember, Crispin, that Jerome is a great success with women as a rule. His experience of serving wenches is that they're delighted to be kissed and fondled by the Quality! And though Peri isn't like that, she's got a very twinkly, cuddly way with her. I understand from Selina that even Tufton—and he's a sober citizen, you'll agree—was quite carried away.'

'Yes, he was,' admitted Lord O'Neill, sitting down again. 'What am I to do, Mamma? She's the sweetest child, and ...'

'I think she should be married off before she's seduced and ruined,' Lady O'Neill said bluntly. 'Oh, I know village girls do bear children to the nobility and then marry a man of their own class, but Peri deserves better than that. I was wondering about Arnold Ledsham? He's a tenant farmer, but the farm is right on the edge of the estate, and he's unmarried and hunting for a wife.'

'What's that got to do with it? That his farm is on the edge of the estate?' his lordship asked suspiciously.

Lady O'Neill looked surprised. 'Why, nothing, except that if you suggested he marry the girl, then it would be proper to give the farm as a dowry. Otherwise what inducement would there be for him to marry her?'

'Judging by the number of people who've tried to kiss Peri, fondle her legs, pinch her bottom and so on, all we need do is take her over to Ledsham's place and leave him alone with her for half an hour,' Lord O'Neill said, grinning. 'She's an inducement in herself, the little devil! Of course, I would give him the farm, only ...'

'Only what?'

'Well, I did buy Peri for ... for the girls, you know. I'm damned if I want to see her married off to a horny-handed farmer just because she's pretty and seductive without ever meaning to be! Look, how would it be if I put the fear of death into Jerome, and had a word with old Prothero? You know what butlers are, if I tell him I'll have his hide if the girl's molested, she'll be safe enough.'

'I think Peri can handle the servants without any help,' Lady O'Neill said, her mouth quirking into a smile. 'It's those who are supposed to be her social superiors whom it is difficult to refuse. Jerome, in other words. He is enormously powerful physically, and used to getting his way with women.'

'I'll deal with him,' her son said.

Lady O'Neill, seeing the white line around his mouth, said apprehensively, 'No violence, Crispin!' very much as she had done when he was a small and aggressive boy.

He turned to grin at her. 'No violence, Mamma!' he promised, and was gone.

Upon quitting his mother's boudoir, Lord O'Neill walked towards the stairs, wondering how he was to detach Jerome from Pamela's society in order to hand out a strongly worded warning. However, he must do it, and furthermore he would tell Jerome that if he intended to offend again he would no longer be welcome at Brownlow Hall. This, he thought, should do the trick, since Jerome made no secret of the fact that he enjoyed the hunting and shooting parties which the family held later in the year. His lordship was also shrewd enough to realise that it was beneath the roof of Brownlow Hall, where he was welcomed as a cousin and his libertine propensities ignored, that Jerome stood the best chance of meeting the heiress he needed to repair his fortunes.

He had reached the head of the stairs and was hesitating, wondering where he would find Jerome and Pamela, when Peri came swiftly across the hall and ran up the stairs, her steps light. Immediately, his lordship was aware of a desire to talk things over with Peri. After all, if she truly desired to marry Arnold Ledsham and become a farmer's wife, then he would not stand in her way.

She reached the top of the stairs and saw him. A beaming smile spread across her face. 'Oh! I've eaten my supper, and I was going back to your Mamma, sir.'

'Well, don't. No, wait, you've tasks in her dressing-room, haven't you?' At her nod he concluded, 'Good. I'll come with you and we can talk while you iron, or mend or whatever.'

'Yes, that would be very nice,' she said demurely. 'Come in.'

She led him into a small room with gowns, skirts, mantles, wigs and other aids to beauty hanging from every available wall surface, and Peri pulled forward a small three-legged stool and sat down upon it, picking up a petticoat with a torn flounce and beginning to stitch. Then she got up and went across and opened the door which led into the adjoining room. She peeped through, then closed it and returned to her perch.

'I know that your Mamma would not listen,' she said, 'but that wall is thin; I've often lain here at night and heard every word she and Moorfield exchanged.' A twinkling glance told him that *she* had listened! 'But it's all right, your Mamma has gone to Eleanor. She often does about now.'

His lordship, glancing round, saw the edge of a pallet bed sticking out from behind some hanging gowns and guessed she must sleep on that. He pulled it out and perched rather uncomfortably upon the edge.

'Then we can talk. Peri, I want to know how you feel about men.'

As soon as the words were out of his mouth he wondered what on earth had made him utter them.

As if he didn't know! She liked men, but disliked being kissed! That, in a nutshell, was the whole trouble. And men, seeing themselves liked, took kissing for granted!

Peri, however, thought the question a fair one. 'I like *you*,' she said frankly, 'but I don't like Mr Harcourt.'

'You don't like Mr Harcourt because he ... he molested you,' Lord O'Neill began. But the wide eyes turned on him at once.

'It isn't that! If you had kissed me I shouldn't have minded.'

'Ah! Well, the point is ... You see, Peri, it's like this ...' His lordship was floundering, and at the back of his mind a strong feeling of resentment, because he seemed to be the only male in the house who had not kissed Peri, was growing. Her small face was turned up to his now, her lips a little parted, her dark eyes questioning.

'Confound it!' Lord O'Neill said, between clenched teeth. He jumped up from the bed, sending it back against the wall with a thump, reached down and picked Peri off her stool as though she had weighed no more than a kitten. He was aware of an immense satisfaction as he held her, feeling her arms curl round his neck, her body press itself against him, and then he bent his head and their mouths met.

He was amazed by the wave of intoxication which swept through him as his mouth possessed hers. She gave a little murmur of pleasure as he parted her lips, exploring her mouth gently, his increasing desire for her held in check because she would, he knew, have given herself so willingly.

His hands moved possessively over her shoulder blades, down to her slight waist, meeting the heavy skirt and petticoat yet feeling through her clothing the small hip bones, the line of her thigh. Without realising it he had moved forward, carrying her into the gowns which hung from the wall. His hands were quiet now, resting on her hips, yet she made no attempt to move away, clinging to him, quiescent in his arms.

In the semi-darkness amongst the gowns, his scruples disappeared. She was pressed against him, her mouth surrendered for his pleasure, her body, he knew instinctively, his for the taking. He pulled her hips forward and she made a soft little sound of satisfaction as his lips began their slow, warm journey down the soft skin of her neck, across the tender hollows, down to the swell of her breasts. Somehow, without quite knowing how, she was half under him, he was kneeling over her, his lips hot against the cool skin of her upper breasts.

And then some last fragment of sanity made him open his eyes. He saw her, half-sitting, half-lying, her eyes closed, her lips trembling, waiting for him. And he saw his own hands on her skin, knew that in another moment he would have gone too far—*he*, who had despised his cousin Jerome for kissing her!

He said, 'Dear God, I must be insane,' and then, because she still looked dazed with pleasure, he kissed her gently, coolly, before lifting her to her feet.

Her face was deep pink and she murmured, 'Why? Oh, I love you so, sir! Why?'

Lord O'Neill, still wanting her most urgently, said huskily, 'I must have been mad. You're only a child!'

She looked up at him, wide-eyed. 'Have you never had a mistress?'

His lordship thought of Veronica Browning, who had taught him a great deal when he was in his teens; he thought of Cathy Skelton, an actress who performed divinely, both on the stage and in his bed. He swallowed. Neither Veronica nor Cathy could hold a candle to Peri, he knew that!

'Yes, I've had mistresses. But they were older than you, more experienced. And they weren't ... they weren't ...'

'Are you worried because you would be my first man? But there must *be* a first, mustn't there?'

His lordship sighed. 'Oh, Peri! I don't want you to be like that! You're a beautiful innocent. One day you'll want to marry. Do you want to take damaged goods to your marriage bed?'

She shook her head. 'I shan't want to marry. And for a moment, you *did* want me.' She leaned against him, looking up into his face, and it was all he could do not to draw her back into his arms and damn the consequences. 'Is it that I'm too young to be a good mistress?'

'Yes, that's it. When you're older ...' He realised what he was saying and gave her a quick hug. 'No, you don't know what you're saying, I mean ...'

'Just what do you mean, Crispin?'

Jerome stood there, his dark face inscrutable in the failing light.

'Good God, you startled me,' his lordship said. 'I've just been telling Peri ...'

'*Telling* her? By the look of it, you've been showing her! So you wanted her for yourself, did you? Trying to make me feel small, talking about your responsibilities, when all the time you'd planned a nice, cosy little seduction in here!'

'I'd planned nothing of the sort,' his lordship returned crisply. 'I've been telling Peri about our plans ...' For the life of him he could not go on lying, with Jerome's scornful eyes on him and Peri, still with her gown half off one shoulder and that tell-tale glow in her eyes, standing so close.

'Just wait until Pamela hears!'

'I've done her no harm,' Lord O'Neill found himself saying defensively. 'A kiss ...'

'I've done some kissing myself, but my ... er ... partner doesn't usually have such a rumpled appearance,' Jerome drawled.

Peri, looking from face to face, said suddenly, 'Yes, Mr Harcourt, it *was* only a kiss. And very much I liked it! Don't *dare* talk in that ugly way to Milord, or I'll ... I'll kill you!'

For some reason that she could not understand, the atmosphere, which had been charged with animosity, suddenly relaxed. Lord O'Neill said, a little stiffly still, 'You were right to upbraid me, Jer, but I promise you I'd already apologised to Peri. And now we'd best leave the child to get on with her work.'

It was at that point that the adjoining door opened, and Lady O'Neill came into the room.

'Quite a little party, I see,' she remarked pleasantly, looking from one face to the other. 'But you're neglecting your sister and Miss Courtney, Crispin, you'd best join the ladies. And you, Jerome. You'll find them in the crimson salon, playing and singing at the piano.'

'Very well, Mamma,' his lordship said, colouring to the roots of his hair. He glanced at Jerome, and was pleased to see that saturnine and sophisticated rake also looking rather red about the gills. 'We'll join the ladies, eh, coz?'

As soon as they had gone her ladyship turned to Peri and scanned the younger girl keenly. Peri had hitched her dress back into position and pushed back her tumbled locks, but Lady O'Neill could still read the message in the flushed cheeks, the bright eyes, the too-rosy lips. *That child has been kissed, and enjoyed it thoroughly,* was her first thought. But who? Then her mind went back to her son's face, as she had seen it when she had first opened the door. He had glanced briefly down at Peri while she made her impassioned declaration, and she remembered clearly the tenderness in his eyes. It might mean nothing at all, she told herself. Or it might mean a good deal. It would be best, perhaps, to take certain steps.

'Peri, dear, what is your name? Your real name?'

'Rachelle Blanche Nicolette Perigand,' Peri reeled off, grimacing.

'I see. And your father's name?'

'Jean-Claude Perigand.'

'Well dear, thank you for telling me. But I think perhaps Crispin was right, and Peri is easier for us to remember. For now, at any rate.' Her glance roved round the room and came to rest on the space where Peri and Lord O'Neill had pushed gowns and petticoats off their hooks as they kissed. 'Dear me, that skirt is crumpled! And my green Italian silk has been knocked to the floor. Just get out the iron, dear, and smooth them out for me.'

Peri, with a martyred sigh, did as she was told. But even the hated task of ironing could not take the brilliance out of her eyes or the warm glow from her heart.

The day after the scene in the dressing-room, Lord O'Neill felt rather foolish in upbraiding Jerome for his behaviour at the lodge, but Jerome took it in good part, only having one stab at his lordship in return.

'I quite agree, old fellow, that I ought not to have kissed the child, and I know you feel the same—and you weren't bitten damn' nearly to the bone. But does it occur to you that you're behaving very like a dog in a manger? You don't want her yourself, but you don't want anyone else to have her either!'

'That isn't so. If a decent man comes forward and wants to marry her ...'

'Is it likely? She's a *slave*, man! You'll have to free her before she can marry, and you've not done that yet.'

'She doesn't want to marry yet. She's too young.'

'She doesn't want to marry because she knows

only a yokel would take her for a bride,' Jerome returned brutally. 'She'd be your mistress though, wouldn't she? Or mine, if I bought her from you, which I would, and for twice what you paid.' He grinned at the ugly look which suddenly transformed his cousin's normally handsome features. 'No need to look like murder, Crispin! It was no sin when you bought her. It seems to me you've no use for her, and I have! Once she was mine, I'd soon bring her round to the idea of being my mistress. A few kisses, caresses, and she'd come round.' He grinned. 'Women always do!'

Lord O'Neill turned his shoulder on his cousin and strode out of the room. But he was an honest young man, and was uneasily aware that there was more than a grain of truth behind Jerome's gibes. He was no moralist and had enjoyed several mistresses, it was just that since he intended asking Pamela to be his wife he could scarcely take an innocent child like Peri to his bed.

He went down to the crimson salon and found Eleanor there alone, playing the piano. He stayed with her for a little while, feeling increasingly miserable, and wondering what Jerome would say to Pamela. And then he told his sister that he was going out for a ride, and left the house.

Jerome, meanwhile, had decided to tell Miss Courtney everything. If she saw she was losing his lordship to a slave-girl, it might do one of two things. It might make her throw herself at Crispin's head, or it might make her turn to himself. He devoutly hoped it would be the latter!

He found her in the book-room, and suggested a stroll in the grounds. She accepted with an alacrity he might have found flattering at any other time, but now his mind was on how he should best tell his story. And in the event, he found he scarcely had to say more than a few words before she had flown into a rage, her eyes flashing blue fire, her lips tight.

'That trollop!' she hissed. 'If he's so hot for a woman, why doesn't he take her, and have done?'

Jerome found himself, for the first time in his life, a little shocked. His mouth opened and shut but no words came out.

'He's going to offer for *me*,' Miss Courtney said insistently, 'I know he is! He adores me, he's wildly in love with me, yet … the way he looks at her … Oh, how hateful men can be!'

She had whirled round at that point and left him flat, running into the house as if the devil himself were after her. And I had not even begun to make my point, Jerome thought, aggrieved. He wondered very much what such an impetuous young lady would do next!

Lord O'Neill could have told him. Crossing the stableyard, intent on his ride, a voice hailed him.

'Crispin, darling! You've been saying you wanted to ask me something ever since the wedding! They told me in the house that you'd ordered Rambler to be saddled, so I've left poor Jerome throwing dice, right hand against left, and I've had Serenade saddled too. I'll come riding with you, and then you can ask me whatever you like!'

Miss Courtney stood there, her faultless figure

clad in a dark blue riding habit, reflecting and seeming to darken the blue of her eyes. A small blue hat
was perched on the shining crown of her hair and
there was a blue ribbon tied round the handle of her
whip.

Reluctantly, he turned towards her. God, what
moments women chose! Just when he was full of
doubts and misery this golden creature, who had had
his thoughts and dreams in her keeping for the past
year, must needs decide to hear the proposal which
had hovered on his lips ever since his return to
England!

'Riding? Yes, I was going riding,' he said. 'To ...
to see my aunts. I'd be delighted with your company,
of course.'

Later that afternoon, Miss Courtney entered Brownlow Hall on a wave of excitement, her voice a little
too high, her cheeks a little too flushed. She tripped
across the hall and entered the crimson salon where
Eleanor, Lady O'Neill and Jerome were sitting,
drinking tea.

'My dear Lady O'Neill,' Miss Courtney cried,
hurrying across the room, 'I know it will come as no
surprise to *you* if I say that very soon I shall beg to be
allowed to call you Mamma! I have accepted
Crispin's offer. I declare, I'm so happy I could
cry!'

His lordship, following his betrothed into the
room, turned a haggard face towards his mother.
'Yes, indeed. My first visit when we arrive in London
must be to Berkeley Square, though Pamela assures

me that Lord Courtney will be delighted by the
news.'

'And not one whit surprised,' Pamela said gaily.
'For you cannot deny that you've danced attendance
on me for the best part of a year, my lord.'

Jerome was not the only one who noticed the
almost threatening quality of that last remark. Nor
the only person to see that Lord O'Neill was by no
means the happy man he tried to appear. Jerome was
conscious of two conflicting emotions. Annoyance
with himself, for having made such a poor job of
telling Miss Courtney about Crispin and Peri, and a
certain satisfaction, for now he would be able to take
the slave-girl without a qualm. Probably Cris would
be glad enough to sell her and make it all legal, he
mused, for he was very sure that in the circumstances
Miss Courtney would never consent to have the girl
in her household.

Lady O'Neill's mind whirled with conjecture. She
had no doubt that Pamela had forced Crispin's
hand, just as she had no idea why. Unless... She had
read something in Crispin's face when he looked
down at Peri the previous evening. Was it possible
that Jerome had done the same, and told Pamela? If
Pamela knew that his lordship was in love with Peri,
she must also have known she herself would have to
move swiftly or lose her most eligible suitor for ever.

As soon as she could, Lady O'Neill left the happy
couple alone and hurried to her room. Moorfield and
Peri were both there, preparing the room for the
night.

'Ah, Moorfield, just the person I wanted to see!

You did despatch James to London with that note for Mr Walpole?'

Moorfield nodded. 'Oh, yes, Milady! He took the mail coach, as you desired, so he'll be there by now. But you wanted him to wait for a reply, which might, perhaps, take a little time.'

There was the trace of a question in her tone but her ladyship merely smiled, saying 'thank you, Moorfield', and sending Peri downstairs with a message that she would like to speak to Miss Courtney as soon as was convenient.

Within the space of a very few minutes Miss Courtney was at the door, for she was far too well brought up to keep her hostess waiting. She entered the room with her usual grace, saying sweetly, 'Your maid says you want to see me, Lady O'Neill', but behind the smooth façade of ease, her ladyship could sense her young guest's wariness.

'My dear, your betrothal to my son gives me great happiness, but you realise that until your father's consent has been obtained you must not, to put it vulgarly, "puff it off"? It could lead to great embarrassment.'

Pamela, after a thoughtful pause, agreed to tell no one but her closest friends.

'No, Pamela, not even your closest friends. There can be no notice sent to the *Williamsons Advertiser* nor to the London *Gazette*. Between ourselves, my dear, this betrothal does not exist—cannot exist—until your Papa's consent has been asked for and received.'

In vain did Pamela assure her hostess that her

father's consent was merely a matter of form, that she knew her father had been expecting his lordship to declare himself as soon as he returned from his plantations.

Nevertheless, insisted Lady O'Neill firmly, there could be no word of the betrothal until Lord Courtney's formal consent to the marriage had been received, and at last Pamela was forced, reluctantly, to agree.

When the girl left her, Lady O'Neill sat in a chair by the window, embroidering a piece of tapestry with tiny, swift stitches. She felt she had done her best for her son. The rest she must leave to fate—and Mr Walpole.

CHAPTER
EIGHT

Peri had heard about the betrothal shortly after its announcement. It annoyed, but did not perturb her. For she knew now, that whoever he might marry, Miss Courtney was not the wife for Lord O'Neill.

The thought that his lordship might marry herself had never entered her head. To be near him, to know herself regarded with affection by him, was all she could hope for, but she knew that if he married Miss Courtney, even such crumbs of comfort would be denied her.

Therefore the marriage must not take place. But how to prevent it? It would be useless, obviously, to give his lordship a distaste for marriage to Miss Courtney. Though she had not seen his face when the joyful news had been given, others had. The butler, Mr Prothero, said his lordship looked as though he had lost a guinea and found a groat and the footman described the harassed peer's expression as being akin to 'someone a-chewin' lemons'.

So, since Lord O'Neill had obviously already discovered his mistake, she must see to it that Miss Courtney realised hers. But how? How? She was well aware that it was his lordship's social position and fortune which drew Miss Courtney to him. If she could have reduced Lord O'Neill to penury at one stroke Peri, a determined young woman, would undoubtedly have done so. As it was, she could only chew her underlip as she cleaned Lady O'Neill's diamond-heeled evening slippers, and think furiously.

To give Miss Courtney a distaste for Brownlow Hall seemed the best notion. After all, if she did marry his lordship she would have to live here quite half the year. Yes, that was it. She had toyed previously with the idea of a plague of snakes. Now she must do something! She had managed to discover, in seemingly casual conversation with the head gardener, that there were both adders and grass snakes to be found on the estate at this time of year.

She knew how one captured snakes. A soft cotton bag and a forked stick would be all the equipment she would need, plus keen eyes and a swift hand. In the days when she had lived in Africa, the children had often indulged in snake-hunts, and she had been good at it, better than many of her friends.

She planned her expedition carefully this time. She had no desire to run into Mr Harcourt's arms, though she could not help chuckling over the thought of that gentleman finding his arms full, not only of Peri, but of snakes! However, she made careful enquiries before setting out.

It really seemed, this time, that she would be safe. Though Miss Courtney had announced that the fair was far beneath her, she had consented to a tour of a porcelain manufactory with enthusiasm, especially when Jerome said he would go with the happy couple, and would beg Miss Alison Goodrich, the elder daughter of a neighbour, to accompany them.

Peri, safely tucked away in the loft above the stables, watched the young people set out in the four-wheeled chaise drawn by two handsome black matched stallions. They made a pretty picture, but Peri watched them go without regret. It never occurred to her to envy Miss Courtney her lovely dresses, her rich and secure life. All she envied her was his lordship's love, and now that she was sure he did not love Miss Courtney she cared nothing for the rest.

As soon as she was sure the coast was clear she stole down into the stables, ran across the yard, and plunged into the woods, forked stick at the ready. Her plan was to capture as many snakes as possible and to release one or two of them in Miss Courtney's rooms every few days until Miss Courtney fled the house. She did have a moment's doubt over where she would keep the snakes waiting to be released, but with her usual bright optimism, decided that a solution to the problem would arise once the snakes were captured.

It was cool and shady in the wood, and Peri padded along, her ears pricked for the slightest sound. At last she came to a clearing where pale green bracken fronds were uncurling. From the thick of it came a rustle.

Peri, her stick poised shoulder-high, like a harpoon, stole forward on tiptoe. She was hunting now, her whole mind concentrating on her quarry. The stick hovered, then plunged as Peri struck unerringly into the heart of the bracken, from whence the rustlings came.

There is something very peculiar about this expedition, Miss Courtney thought, *yet I cannot quite put my finger upon it*. Miss Goodrich was a charming girl, a brunette with velvety brown eyes and a plump pretty face. She was friendly and forthcoming towards Miss Courtney and was at ease with both men whom she had known, she gaily informed the other girl, since childhood.

In the chaise she and Miss Goodrich sat side by side, facing the two young men, and it was then that it occurred to Miss Courtney that his lordship was treating her with friendly civility, comradeship even, but definitely not with the eager adoration to which she had become accustomed.

Piqued, she began to flirt with Jerome, talking about her various beaux, her plans for what was left of the Season—and watching his lordship for the first sign of jealous possessiveness which, surely, would not be long in coming? It did not arrive. His lordship continued pleasant, chatting to herself and Miss Goodrich with impartial good manners.

When the chaise drew up outside the manufactory Jerome and Lord O'Neill jumped down and Miss Courtney, seeing Jerome step forward, politely insisted that Miss Goodrich should descend before her. The other girl did so, was caught by the helpful Jerome, and handed on to his lordship, who promptly offered his arm.

Miss Courtney, following, with her hand tucked into the crook of Jerome's elbow, could only wonder how she had been so neatly out-manoeuvred. She looked scornfully at Miss Goodrich's impervious back, wondering how the other girl could so boldly walk off with a man betrothed to someone else.

Miss Courtney was not slow-witted, however, and before they had gone halfway round the manufactory it occurred to her to wonder what Jerome had told Miss Goodrich. From the other girl's pleasant demeanour, she realised that Miss Goodrich must have been told that Jerome and Miss Courtney were to be one couple, his lordship and herself the other.

It was equally obvious, she realised with increasing annoyance, that though Lord O'Neill may not have been a party to the deception, he was by no means averse to having the unexacting companionship of the other girl. Jerome, too, was pleased with himself. He hung back, forcing her to do the same, and whispered that she looked so pretty when she was angry that had it not been for the plumes on her hat, which got so confoundedly in the way, he would have been unable to stop himself from kissing her soundly!

Miss Courtney, who would have enjoyed the situation if only Lord O'Neill had shown a natural jealousness, found herself helpless. She might—and did—seethe with annoyance, but she was a young lady. She could not tell the world how badly she had been treated. She could only endure.

When, back in the chaise once more, his lordship asked Miss Goodrich to dine with them, and Miss

Goodrich, with a dimpled smile, accepted, Miss Courtney could have screamed with vexation.

'If we could persuade Eleanor to play for us, we might dance,' Miss Goodrich suggested. 'Do you like to dance, Miss Courtney?'

'No!' snapped Miss Courtney. 'I've a headache.'

Her companion, snubbed, turned to the young men and they began an animated three-way discussion on horseflesh which lasted until the stableyard was reached, and then both girls were handed down and taken into the house, where Lady O'Neill promptly bore Miss Goodrich away to her own rooms to wash and tidy before dinner.

Miss Courtney, thoroughly out of temper, went wearily to her chamber. Chapman was there, laying out a particularly beautiful evening dress in primrose silk with a ruched and embroidered train and a gauze scarf, sewn with trembling pearl-drops. She looked up when her mistress came in.

'Och, what an afternoon,' she said sourly. 'I'd barely got that idle scamp, Polly, to bring up fresh coal and wood for the fire than I'd a message from the gardener to go down to the glass-houses for your flowers. But when I got there, no one knew anything about it. The flowers were in the butler's pantry as usual, waiting to be arranged.'

Miss Courtney shrugged, beginning to peel off her long kid gloves.

'I've had a dreadful afternoon,' she said pettishly. 'A horrid, boring trail round the porcelain manufactory, where it was so hot, and then talking to that dull Miss Goodrich in the chaise. We've nothing in common, all she thinks about is horses! And now she's to stay to dinner, so I shall be bored with her for the rest of the evening, I suppose!'

'Aye, but at least there will be the four of you,' Miss Chapman pointed out. 'You and his lordship will be able . . .'

'His lordship has been paying marked attention to Miss Goodrich,' Miss Courtney said, bitterly and untruthfully. 'And Mr Harcourt has scarcely left my side all afternoon. I don't know what's going on! I can't but wonder if Lady O'Neill's a party to it! All that talk about not telling anyone that Crispin and I are betrothed! Such fustian!'

Chapman, seeing her lady so discomposed, immediately set about soothing her. 'Never mind, miss,' she said. 'Just you lie down for half an hour and I'll put a damp cloth on your forehead, and mix you up one of Dr James's powders. Then you'll feel better.'

Tenderly she helped her mistress out of the tobine striped skirt with the tight, laced bodice, hanging up her hoop in the dressing-room. She slipped Miss Courtney into a loose, comfortable negligée and then went into the dressing-room and began to mix a powder with milk.

She was just pouring the concoction into a cut-glass goblet when the most dreadful scream rent the air. For a moment she stood stock still, then she dropped the goblet on to the polished floor, heedless of splintering glass, and rushed to her mistress, whose shrieks had redoubled.

She was not the only one to come running.

Moorfield, Peri and Miss Goodrich had reached the bedroom neck and neck, whereupon Peri prudently held back, allowing Moorfield and Miss Goodrich to burst in, Moorfield crying, 'Mercy, Miss Courtney, what has happened?'

Miss Courtney, shuddering and giving vent to gulping sobs, was leaning against the wall, pointing with a trembling finger to her bed.

'I ... I ... I ... pulled back the ... the ... sheet, and ... oh! Oh! *Oh!*'

The watchers saw a small, bedraggled head appear above the sheets. Beady eyes glanced round cautiously, then a round, prickly body emerged.

'A hedgehog! How on earth ...'

That was Miss Goodrich, her eyes rounding.

Chapman swept forward, her mouth tight as a trap. 'Well! The dirty, disgusting thing! It'll have fleas and all sorts. How on earth did it get in there?'

Peri, after one satisfied glance at her victim, had silently slipped away. She went back to Lady O'Neill's room, for Moorfield was looking after Miss Goodrich, saying casually in reply to her mistress's raised brows, 'A little animal in Miss Courtney's bed. A little round creature. Hedge ... something. I don't know how you say it.'

'In her *bed*? A hedgehog?' Lady O'Neill looked very hard at Peri, but the small face remained blandly innocent.

'I think that's it. Yes, a hedge'og.' Peri moved forward, picking up the hairbrush. 'May I brush your back curls out now, Milady?'

'Peri, how did a hedgehog come to be in Miss

Courtney's bed?' Through the mirror her ladyship saw the shrug, the innocent, faintly puzzled expression. 'Where were you this afternoon?'

Peri, curling a strand of hair expertly round her finger, said, 'I went a walk. I met only Polly, I think, then I had some tea with Mrs Pershore. Why?'

'I see,' Lady O'Neill said meaningly. 'Well, it must not occur again, do you understand?'

Through the mirror, she saw Peri's naughtiest smile. 'No?'

Despite herself, Lady O'Neill smiled back. She shook her head. 'No. And I *mean* no, Peri.' She hesitated, then, because she genuinely wanted to know, she added, 'Why, my child?'

'Because she'll make his lordship unhappy,' Peri declared definitely. 'She is bad, that one. Not good.'

'But he asked her to marry him.'

Peri shook her head. 'No, she teased him into asking her. She made him ashamed. I'm not very old, but I know how it was.'

Lady O'Neill sighed. 'I'm rather afraid you're right. But what difference will a hedgehog in the bed make?'

Through the mirror, Peri cocked an intelligent eye. 'A snake would be better? But I could not find one, for all Jenkins says there are plenty.'

'A *snake*?' Lady O'Neill shrieked. 'Don't you *dare* bring a snake into this house! If you do, I shall see that my son sends you away at once!'

'You don't like them?' Peri caught her ladyship's eye in the mirror, and grinned. 'Very well, I won't bring them indoors. And no more hedges, either.'

'Hedgehogs.'

'Hedgehogs,' Peri repeated obediently. 'Shall I fetch your powdering cape now, Milady?'

In fact, Peri thought afterwards, her expedition in search of snakes had not been a resounding success. First she had stabbed her forked stick into the bracken and disturbed Polly and one of the undergardeners, locked in a passionate embrace. In fact, 'disturbed' was scarcely the word for the feelings of the outraged couple. And Peri herself had been horribly startled by the ardent suitor's howls, and had for one awful moment thought that she had inadvertently speared a sleeping lion.

Then, when explanations had been offered and reluctantly accepted, they had advised her to take herself and her stick into the open, so that she might run no more risk of attacking innocent courting couples.

'For 'tis a miracle that you only got Fred in the be'ind,' Polly said resentfully. 'If you'd not stopped when 'e roared, you could've 'ad me eye out!'

In the circumstances, Peri had not liked to point out that Fred's behind was such a sizeable target that there had been little chance of spearing anything else. Chastened, she went on her way, and her only success had been the small hedgehog, which she had found under a pile of dead leaves in the wood.

When she left Lady O'Neill she had steered clear of Miss Courtney, but whatever the mistress may have thought, her maid soon aired her opinion.

'Nae doubt it was that wee heathen, Peri,' Chapman asserted in the servants' hall. 'Dirty, wretched creature. Jealous of Miss Courtney's pretty looks, no doubt.'

Miss Courtney was not popular in the servants' hall and neither was Chapman, with her constant demands upon the staff and her equally constant complaints.

'Why would Peri do a thing like that?' Polly said, though she, more than anyone, had cause to know what must have happened. 'You've no call to talk like that, Miss Chapman.'

Chapman sniffed, but seeing that popular opinion was against her, ate the rest of her meal in stony silence, repairing to her mistress's room as soon as she had finished.

Peri, coming down late and eating her meal with ferocious speed, congratulating cook on 'the loveliest pudding in the world', found herself very much the centre of attention.

'Why did it have to be me? Why no one else?'

'No one else would 'ave dared,' Polly said. 'She's sharp and nasty for all she's pretty as a picture, that Miss Courtney.'

'You want to be careful,' Moorfield warned her. 'When she's mistress here she'll make your life hell!'

'If you'd all help, and fill her bed with snakes, and send up cold water, and put worms in her salad, then she wouldn't *be* mistress here,' Peri cried desperately. But though there were chuckles and half-admiring shakes of the head, her pleas for help fell on stony ground.

'She's pretty and she's rich,' Rawlins the cook summed it up, 'so I suppose he might do worse.'

'But he doesn't love her, nor she him,' Peri pointed out.

'Ho, love, is it?' Albert squeezed her hand and rolled his eyes at her. 'That's for the likes of you an' me, Peri me darlin'! The Quality 'as better reasons for marrying than love. They take mistresses for love and wives for money, and heirs.'

Peri nodded thoughtfully. 'I see. But it would be better for us if he married a nice wife, wouldn't it?'

This innocent observation was received with incredulous guffaws. For who, as several people remarked, ever considered the servants when planning a wedding? So Peri allowed the matter to drop and decided to go early to bed, and once there, to give her whole mind and invention to the problem.

She was in bed when the scratching came at her door. She slid out of the covers and said cautiously, 'Who is that?'

'Jerome Harcourt. I want to speak to you.'

'Ha!' Peri said scornfully. 'I do not believe that. Go away!'

'It's the truth. Come on, Peri, let me in!'

Peri crossed the room again and climbed back into bed. 'Shan't. Did you hear me getting back into bed? Well, now I shall go to sleep, and if you make a big noise you'll wake the 'ousekeeper. She'll send you off with a flea in your hair.'

'In your *ear*, Peri, not in your hair.'

'What?'

She heard him sigh, then he shifted uneasily, but he did not go away. He spoke again, his voice scarcely above a whisper.

'Peri, please! This could mean everything to us both. It's about this marriage.'

Peri sat up in bed again. 'What about it? Whisper to me. I'm listening.'

'I think I know a way to prevent it. Now will you come out?'

Sorely tempted, Peri still retained enough common sense to say with an assumption of firmness, 'No. Why can't you tell me in the morning?'

She thought she could *hear* him grin; she could imagine so well the white teeth flashing in the dark, the reluctant amusement dawning in the heavily lidded eyes.

'Oh very well, you young devil! Can you meet me at six, in the stables?'

'Why not somewhere respectable?'

He gave a chuckle, bitten off short. 'There's nothing disreputable about the stables! And if you're ...' he stopped. 'Someone's coming. To-morrow, at six!'

Peri heard his footsteps creak rapidly away just as other, lighter footsteps crossed the room next to her own. A pause, a door opening softly, and then Polly's voice breathed against the panelling, 'You all right, Peri?'

Peri sighed. She got out of bed, unbolted her door and faced the other girl in the faint light.

'Yes, I'm all right. I didn't unbolt my door.'

Polly's eyebrows climbed. 'Then it was a man? I thought it was!' Her voice sharpened. 'Not Fred?'

'Of course not!' Peri said, affronted. 'Why should Fred come to my room? Unless he is still angry with me because I prodded him with my stick? Which would not be fair, for I said I was sorry.' She scowled at Polly. 'Would he come to my room to punish me for prodding him? If he does, I shall teach him a lesson!'

'I wasn't thinking of . . . Oh, I don't know what I was thinking. Sorry, Peri. Goodnight.'

Peri, bidding Polly goodnight, bolted her door again and climbed back into bed. For a moment she wondered why on earth Polly had thought Fred might have been at her door. After all, she had not meant to spike him with her stick. And since, judging by what she had seen in the bracken, Polly and Fred were much more than friends, she could not imagine that he would seek her out for anything other than revenge.

Snuggling down beneath the blankets again, she decided she would never understand the English. And she also decided she would visit the stables at six o'clock. It would be worth having to put up with Jerome's horrid kisses if he really had a plan to prevent the marriage.

At six o'clock the day was bright and fair, pale early sunshine pouring through the windows of the still sleeping hall and flooding the stableyard with unearthly radiance. Peri, true to her word, went straight to the stables and found Jerome waiting for her.

And this, she could see at a glance, was a very different Jerome from the one who had pursued her so relentlessly before.

'Peri! Good, you've come. If you hadn't ... But where can we talk?'

'Shall we walk in the woods?' Peri suggested. 'Only ...' she produced from the pocket in her apron a kitchen knife, old but sharp.

Jerome blinked, then gave a shout of laughter. 'Good God! Is that to ensure my good behaviour? Will I get it between the ribs if I try to kiss you?'

She nodded, her small face grave. 'Yes, for this marriage is serious, and we are to have a serious talk.'

'Very well. But come into the wood, I don't want to be seen from the house.'

Once in the shelter of the woods, Jerome found a fallen tree, mossy but dry after three days of sunshine, and sat down upon it. Peri seated herself a foot further along, her eyes fixed on his face.

'Well?' she enquired. 'How can you stop the marriage? And why do you want to?'

'Because Miss Courtney is immensely rich and I'm not,' Jerome said frankly. 'I think we should both put our cards on the table, Peri. Why do *you* want to stop Crispin from marrying her?'

'Because she is bad, and doesn't love him.' She saw his sceptical glance and blushed. 'And because she wouldn't let me stay near his lordship,' she added. 'All I want is to be near him. But her, oho, she would not like that!'

'You're right there,' Jerome admitted. 'Now look, you know his lordship is fond of you. And with good reason; you're a taking little thing.'

Peri saw the gleam of light in his eyes and stiffened defensively, but he laughed, patting her knee. 'No, no, don't poker up! You see, Miss Courtney may not love his lordship, but she's jealous of you. If she were to surprise you in a compromising situation with Crispin, and there were witnesses—say myself, Miss Goodrich, or one of the aunts—I'm sure she would break off her betrothal.'

'And then what would happen?'

Jerome smiled a little maliciously. 'Well, he certainly wouldn't feel bound to marry a slave, my dear!' Then, seeing her puzzled glance, he had the grace to look ashamed of himself, saying quickly, 'Why, his lordship would be free! He could look about him for another wife!'

'Yes, that would be very good,' Peri said decidedly. 'Except ... What means compromising situation, sir?'

Jerome bit back the immediate response which rose to his lips and searched for a more delicate way of putting the same thing.

'Well, he would be discovered making love to you,' he said slowly, at last. 'You would have to be a little ... disarranged, to make it look convincing, Peri. Your gown off your shoulder, as it was in the dressing-room the other evening, and your hair tumbled down out of its knot.'

'I see,' Peri said. A doubtful look crossed her small face. 'But would his lordship mind being seen with me ... disarranged?'

'He'd be delighted to be caught with his ... with his arms around you,' Jerome assured her mendaciously. 'He'll be saved from the marriage, won't he?'

'Ye—es,' Peri agreed. 'And what will you do, sir?'

'Comfort Miss Courtney. To the extent of winning her confidence and her hand, if I'm clever,' Jerome said promptly. 'I dare say you'll find this difficult to believe, Peri, but Miss Courtney finds my kisses very· exciting indeed, though she intends to marry Crispin! Now the next question is where?'

'Where?'

'Where shall you seduce my cousin?'

'Would the stables do? Oh, what means ...'

'Seduce,' Jerome said hastily, 'means to kiss and cuddle. All right? No, the stables wouldn't do, it isn't a place Pamela goes often.'

'Milady's powder-room?' Peri suggested after a thoughtful pause. 'She does not go there except to be powdered, of course. It is often empty. Would that do?'

'We—ell, I can't imagine what excuse I would have for taking Pamela in there,' Jerome demurred. 'Tell you what, how about his lordship's study? He's often there in the afternoons.'

'Very well, then. Shall I do it this afternoon, about two o'clock?'

'Excellent.' Jerome smiled at her. 'I'll hang about to make sure you're both in there and we'll make our appearance about ten minutes later. Will that be time enough?'

Peri, remembering the speed with which she and his lordship had descended into the gowns in Milady's dressing-room, could not help thinking that ten minutes would be ample.

And so it was agreed and the conspirators separated, Peri to run indoors to make up her mistress's breakfast tray, Jerome to stroll round to the stables and plan his own part in the campaign.

Once the die had been cast, Peri found herself unaccountably nervous. She knew she would be saving her idol from a distasteful marriage; the only problem was, would he be grateful, or annoyed with her for her interference? Several times she came near to seeking Jerome's company and telling him she would not do it, but despite these misgivings, two o'clock found her outside his lordship's study, hand raised to scratch upon the door panels.

'Come in!'

She slipped into the room, shutting the door behind her.

Lord O'Neill was sitting behind the desk, his head in his hands, studying a formidably fat ledger, but he looked up as she entered, his face lightening.

'Peri! What can I do for you, my child?'

Peri had planned the next part. She walked round the desk, cast herself on to his lordship's chest, and said, in a voice choked with tears, 'Don't marry her, my lord! Oh, don't! She'll send me away, I'll never see you again, and . . .'

'What's all this? Nonsense, no one shall send you away.'

She was clinging to him, arms round his neck, her eyes fixed on his.

'Love me, my lord,' she said huskily. 'Oh, do love me!'

It was an invitation impossible to resist. He pulled her on to his lap, bent his head and kissed her, deepening the kiss as his hands began, urgently, to caress her. He pushed impatiently at the top of her gown and knew no surprise but only satisfaction at finding she wore no stays, so that his hand slipped easily down to cradle her firm young breast, feeling the nipple hardening in his palm as his caresses roused her. She was lying across his lap, warm and supple in his arms, and he knew that this time, he would make her his. His heart was beating so loudly that he could hear nothing but its thunder, his nostrils were full of her skin-scent, his mouth tasted her sweetness.

And then, quite quietly, a voice said, 'Crispin!'

He dragged his mouth away from Peri's, and it was as difficult as anything he had ever done. He looked up, over the soft, tumbled hair.

In the doorway, faces stared at him. Jerome, saturnine, giving nothing away. Pamela, her face white with shock and fury. And his mother. Her face was pale, but she looked composed.

He stood up, lowering Peri carefully to the ground. His face flushed darkly and Peri, looking up at him, saw that he was terribly ashamed.

She knew the part she must play, but she could not

bear his humiliation. 'He has seduced me because I wanted him to,' she said breathlessly. 'That is why, because I begged him to!'

'Seduced her?' Miss Courtney's voice came out dry, throaty with shock. 'Good God, you propose marriage to me one day and seduce a slave the next! What kind of a man *are* you?'

Lord O'Neill swung Peri round to face him. He pulled her gown into position and pushed the hair back from her face, looking hard into her eyes. 'I seduced you?'

'Yes, you did, I swear it. But I asked you to!'

'You lying little jade!' He flung her from him, turning on his heel to walk over towards the group of people still riveted in the doorway. 'I take it, Pamela, that our betrothal is at an end?'

Miss Courtney, still white with rage, said icily, 'It is,' and turned on her heel. Lady O'Neill after one quick, perplexed glance first at her son and then at Peri, followed her guest, leaving Jerome and his lordship in the study with Peri.

Lord O'Neill would not look at her; instead he looked at Jerome. He said in a low, incredulous undertone, 'She *planned* that scene, Jer! I tell you she planned, in cold blood, to have my mother walk in here and find me ... Dear God, she made it all so easy for me.' He laughed, bitterly. 'She's not wearing her stays; it would have been too bad if I'd not been able to get at her for a pair of stays!'

Abruptly, he walked over to Peri, catching her wrist in an iron grip. 'Here, Jer, she's yours! Don't think I'll interfere if you want to make her your whore, for she's little else. No need to pay me, you can have her.' He pushed Peri towards his cousin and as she turned to him, her eyes staring wildly, he added, 'Did you think to entrap me, you little fool?' He turned away, shaking his head. 'She seemed so young, so innocent,' he murmured, more to himself than to either of them. Then he strode out of the room.

Jerome took a step towards the small, still figure, his expression rueful.

'It's all right, child, he'll get over it! He must know you meant him no harm. It's the shame of being caught in the act, and by his own mother.'

Peri turned a small, white face towards him. 'But . . . you brought his mother. You *knew*. Why?'

'Because I wanted the marriage broken! She'll not back down after this! Look, we've done what we set out to do, so no more foolishness. By this time tomorrow he'll know he owes you his freedom, and he'll forgive you for making him look . . . well, like he did look.'

She looked at him, but he had the uneasy feeling that she had not heard a word, and the big eyes seemed to stare blindly.

'Peri! Come on, child! The world hasn't come to an end!'

'He'll send me away,' she said dully. 'He'll sell me. He'll never forgive me.'

Jerome caught her arm, shaking it gently. 'Don't be a goose. He only tried to give you to me because he was hurt and upset. And I won't take you, because

Pamela wouldn't allow it. Just wait, child, until it blows over.'

But Peri, going on lagging steps up to her room, neither answered nor heeded him. She had seen the scorn in his lordship's blue eyes, the curl of disgust on lips which had, minutes earlier, been softly and lovingly kissing hers.

She had lived through terrifying times, under terrible conditions, and she had known great despair and unhappiness.

But never before had she longed so desperately for death.

CHAPTER
NINE

'A storm in a teacup,' Moorfield said roundly. 'Get on with your work, girl! Of course his lordship was wrong to be kissing you, and especially when he's just got betrothed to Miss Courtney. But you needn't look like that!'

Peri took her ironing and mending into the little dressing-room, and when Moorfield went down to have her meal, she remained where she was. She scarcely knew how to bear her own company, and could not face the thought of seeing the curious looks on the faces of her fellow servants.

Presently she heard her mistress enter her boudoir. Lady O'Neill moved around, making up the fire, probably putting on a pair of comfortable slippers. Peri knew she should go to her, but she remained where she was, shrunk into a small heap in the corner, dumb with misery.

Presently, there was a tap on her ladyship's door and Lord O'Neill's beloved voice said, 'Mamma? You wanted to see me?'

'Yes, my son. Come in, and close the door.'

More small sounds; footsteps, creakings. Peri knew that mother and son were seated now, in the armchairs on either side of the hearth.

'Well, Crispin?'

The silence grew heavy between them. Then his lordship said in a low voice, 'I was wrong to throw all the blame on Peri, Mamma. I acknowledge it. Oh, it was carefully planned, but I need not have kissed her, nor ...'

'That isn't important, Crispin. What *is* important is whether you now regard Peri with disgust. And whether you still want to marry Pamela. I dare say if you apologised, Pamela would listen to you. If so, you could visit Lord Courtney and obtain his consent as though the ... the interlude ... in the study had never occurred.'

'I ... don't know,' his lordship said hesitantly.

'I think you *do* know, Crispin.'

The pause spun out again. Peri, sitting up and listening intently, could imagine the pair of them, Lady O'Neill's calm gaze fixed on her son's miserable, guilt-ridden countenance.

'I ... damn it, I *do* know! Until that moment in the study, when she tried to tell the world she'd been seduced, I loved her! I didn't care that she was a slave, Mamma, I loved her! But now my eyes have been opened. She's after what she can get, and small blame to her, but she's not for me. So I'll apologise to Pamela, and I'll sell Peri. Pamela wouldn't have her under the same roof anyway, not after what she saw in the study.'

There was another of those pauses, this time made almost unbearable for Peri by his lordship's deep, uneven breathing. Then Lady O'Neill said gently, 'No, you won't sell her, my son.'

'Marry her off then. Damn it, I'll give her to

young Ledsham, as you suggested. Although I know she's a scheming little trouble-maker, I still can't ... I can't ...'

His voice faded into silence.

'You can't give her in marriage either, Crispin.'

'Can't?' For the first time his voice showed a trace of impatience. 'She's my property, Mamma. My slave! I can do *anything* with her. Damn it, I bought her!'

'Some days ago, Crispin, I wrote to my old friend, Horace Walpole. Today, I had a letter back from him. Miss Rachelle Perigand, daughter of Jean-Claude Perigand, has a great many relatives in France, including a Marquis who is eager to repay her purchase price and set her up as the young lady she, in fact, is.'

There was a stunned silence on both sides of the dressing-room door.

'A Marquis? She's gently born?' His lordship's voice rose. 'What shall I *do*, Mamma?'

Her ladyship's voice had a smile in it. 'I suggest you marry her, my son.'

'*Marry* her? Just because she said I had seduced her? Good God, Mamma, she's still a scheming little wretch, even if she comes of a good family. You aren't suggesting that I must marry her, because she's of good family and claims I seduced her?'

But Peri had slipped out of the dressing-room and was making her way as fast as she could to her own little attic.

Her heart was beating feverishly in her breast.

What did it mean? She had relatives, alive, in France?

But the only words which mattered, were his lordship's. '*Marry* her? Just because she said I'd seduced her?'

Was it possible that her ladyship was telling the truth? That she, Rachelle Perigand, had relatives in France who would take care of her? And because of that, Lord O'Neill might be forced to marry her?

With a little sob, Peri took her cloak down from the hook on the back of the door and changed her soft shoes for a pair of stout boots. She would not stay here to see his lordship forced into marriage with her just because of a few kisses! Another sob rose in her throat as she forlornly faced the truth. She *was* a scheming wretch. She *had* schemed with Jerome, and though she had meant merely to release his lordship from an entanglement which she was sure must be distasteful, she had hurt him terribly. It was best that she go away.

For a moment she considered staying, trying to find out more about these French relatives. But she knew so little about the moral code of these people among whom she lived. Apparently it was all right to seduce a little slave; no one would think any the worse provided you apologised to the lady you were betrothed to. But if the little slave turned out to be a lady ...

She sniffed, and wiped her nose on her sleeve in a thoroughly unladylike manner. No matter, she would manage. She always had.

She slipped down the stairs, silent as the shadows. They must be still talking, Lord O'Neill and his mamma. And then, from his lordship's study, she heard voices.

'You really are going then, Jerome? I'll miss you.'

That was the horrible Miss Courtney, sounding quite regretful.

'Let us hope, beautiful one, that absence will make the heart grow fonder! Yes, I'm going back to London. It has never been my custom to dance attendance on a woman with no hope of . . . a reward . . . and I don't intend to change my ways now. And anyway, with me out of the way, you may decide to make my cousin the happiest man on earth. He is such an eligible match isn't he, Pamela?'

'Yes,' Miss Courtney said, almost unwillingly, it seemed. 'But . . . but . . .'

'But how much pride can a female swallow? I really don't know. You must write and tell me. And we'd best say goodbye now, since I shall be off at the crack of dawn, long before you open those beautiful eyes.'

'Yes.' There was a pause and then Miss Courtney said in a low voice, 'I wish you would not go, Jerome.'

He gave a crack of hard laughter. 'You'd like to have your cake and eat it, wouldn't you? Well, I'm not a cake which you'd find easy to swallow, my dear, for I wouldn't allow you to work off your whims on me! I must go now, or I'll get no sleep before I leave. Farewell, cold heart.'

Peri heard a rustle, then the sound of a kiss, then

Jerome's deep laugh. 'There! Something to remember me by, when you're decorously pecked by your betrothed, if he becomes your betrothed once more!'

Peri waited no longer. So Jerome was leaving! She scuttled across the hall and out to the stables. Very well, she would steal a lift! He need never know, for his coach was roomy and comfortable, with a sizeable box on the back for luggage. She would find somewhere to hide.

She made her way into the coach house and prowled round Jerome's vehicle. Sure enough, the luggage boot was packed, but there was ample room in it for one small girl, curled up with a rug over her. There were rugs in plenty inside the vehicle, she would remove one of them and hide beneath it.

It would be uncomfortable of course, but Peri had no intention of staying there for the duration of the journey to London. She would wait until he stopped to change horses, and then she would climb out and beg or steal a lift in some other conveyance. And when she reached a sizeable town she would work at an inn or as a maid in a private house. Eventually she would make her way to London and try to find Selina. She had no doubt that the kindly Mrs Mapp would help her.

She glanced round the coach house in the dim light. It might be more comfortable to sleep in one of the carriages until morning. But, upon reflection, she decided that she might sleep so soundly that she would awaken to broad daylight and Jerome

Harcourt long gone. Accordingly she fitted herself as neatly as possible into the luggage boot, pulled the rug over herself, and settled down to a long, miserable vigil.

But despite her unhappiness she was a healthy young creature, and needed her sleep. Within ten minutes of climbing into the luggage boot, Peri was in the land of dreams.

She awoke to motion. Horrid, jerky, sick-making motion. But even as her stomach lurched, she felt triumphant. She was on her way, and undiscovered! She risked a peep out of the luggage boot and saw the road fairly hurtling by beneath her. Shuddering slightly, she crouched back in her refuge. At least, she comforted herself, she was saving poor Lord O'Neill from having to marry her out of a misplaced sense of chivalry. Unaccountably, the tears rose to her eyes at that thought. For a moment she was tempted to jump out and run back the way she had come. I would have made him such a good wife, she told herself forlornly. I would have been so good, so loving!

But it was not to be. He would have resented being forced into marriage by a trick of birth. No, Miss Courtney was beautiful and fashionable and would know how to be the lady of Brownlow Hall. She would not be ignorant of powder and hoops and all the niceties of fashion. She would know what might be done and what might not; she would know how to speak to the servants and how to order the sort of dinner his lordship preferred.

I would only have been a nuisance to him, Peri thought miserably. I would have said the wrong thing, done the wrong thing, worn the wrong thing. All I know is how to love him, and how to please him, and those are things anyone can learn. Even Miss Courtney.

The coach was spinning along, the match bays pulling strongly. From under her blanket Peri watched the sun come up, a round red ball, and paint the pale sky with streaks of gold and tangerine. And then because she was unhappy, and felt sick, she fell asleep and dreamed she was back on the *Snow Tempest* on the dreadful voyage from Africa to the Sugar Islands, and whimpered in her sleep.

Lord O'Neill woke to find his valet pulling back the curtains.

'Lovely morning, sir,' Gibbs said, as sunshine streamed into the room.

'Lovely,' his lordship agreed, not, for a moment, remembering why this morning was so particularly lovely, but knowing that his whole body glowed with well-being and that for the first time for many days, he felt an anticipatory thrill at what the day might bring.

Then he remembered. Peri! He had known even before the scene in the study that he loved her and only her. After his first furious renunciation of the idea of marrying the little brat, he had been so full of it that he and his mother had sat up half the night, talking of nothing else. His wonderful Mamma! She told him that she had seen the love in his face when he looked at Peri long before he had dreamed of such a thing himself.

'She had such an *air* that I could not believe her base-born,' she told him, 'so I wrote to Mr Horace Walpole and begged him to tell me what he could discover. He replied very quickly. Peri's uncle, the Marquis de Marne, had been searching for his niece ever since news of the death of his younger brother, Jean-Claude Perigand, reached him.

'At first they believed the child must have been killed by the Negroes when they fled the plantation, though the Marquis still refused to give up hope. But then a rumour began to circulate that a Portuguese trader was making enquiries. He was searching for a white girl, Rachelle Perigand, who was to have been married to him, except that she had disappeared from amongst the tribe who had brought her up.

'Of course, this news greatly excited the Marquis and he thought at once of the slave trade, and caused enquiries to be made in Jamaica. He had, in fact, got news that she might have been sent on to England, and intended travelling to this country as soon as his agent sent back word that a white girl had been sold as a slave, in Liverpool.'

'I must go to her,' Lord O'Neill had said. 'I must tell her that she's got relatives. And that I love her and want to marry her.'

'Not tonight,' Lady O'Neill protested gently. 'Speak to her in the morning, Crispin. And if I were you, I should apologise first for calling her a schemer.'

She had then gone on to tell him how Peri had tried to break up his betrothal to Miss Courtney not for her own sake, but for his.

'The poor little soul never dreamed for one moment that you might marry her. And if she schemed to be found in your arms in the study, it was merely so that you might win your release from Pamela, and not so that she could entrap you,' she concluded rather severely.

'Then why may I not go to her at once? Poor baby, I dare say she's cried herself to sleep.'

'Because she needs to sleep to see things in proportion, before she is faced with this news. First thing tomorrow, I promise you, I'll call her to my room. Then I'll send Moorfield along to call you, and I shall go downstairs, leaving you to make your peace with the child. How will that be?'

And now, at last, it was morning. Crispin marvelled that he had managed to sleep at all, let alone so soundly, and startled Gibbs by suddenly hurling back the bedclothes and jumping out of bed.

'I'm going to propose marriage this morning, Gibbs,' he announced cheerfully, 'so get me shaved and dressed in record time, if you please.'

'Yes, sir,' Gibbs said, adding, a shade reproachfully, 'but you proposed marriage three days ago, to my certain knowledge!'

Taken aback, his lordship stared, then chuckled. 'So I did! By God, I'm going it a bit, eh? My previous betrothal, however, is at an end. This time I shall propose to Peri. That is, I should say Miss Rachelle Perigand, I suppose.'

The valet's thin face creased into an enormous smile. 'I'm glad, sir. She's a real little lady, for all she's a slave.'

This remark pleased his lordship enormously, and the bedecking of his person in his best coat and breeches, his shaving and the brushing and pomading of his fair curls, was beguiled by Lord O'Neill telling his valet the romantic story which his mother had unfolded to him only a few hours previously.

In fact, Lord O'Neill had only just straightened his stock, brushed an imaginary speck of dust off his shoulder, and said, 'All tidy, Gibbs?' when the knock sounded.

'That'll be Moorfield, to tell me Peri's waiting,' his lordship said, hurrying eagerly to the door.

He opened it and sure enough, Moorfield stood outside. But her face was pale, her eyes wide, one hand clutched at her throat.

'She's gone, sir!'

'Gone?' He was past her, making for the attic stairs. 'She's in her room. Must be!'

Moorfield, close behind him, was half sobbing, 'No sir, no! Her bed hasn't been slept in. She's gone, I tell you!'

He ignored her, taking the stairs two at a time, bursting into the little room which he remembered as being the first on the right at the top of the stairs, though he had never visited it. He never gave a thought to Moorfield's suspicions being aroused by his knowing the room and in this he was right, for Moorfield was far too stunned by Peri's disappearance to read anything into his lordship's unerring entry into the right room.

His lordship, standing in the middle of the bare little room, felt a lump in his throat. His gaze flicked over a Sunday gown hanging on a hook, a pair of scuffed slippers beside the bed, and a bunch of wild flowers in an old jar on the window-sill. He saw the bed, neatly made with its thin blankets, and the low little window, wedged open at the top with a piece of wood so that the fresh air could come in. His love had lived here for weeks, and he had not known what a poor place it was!

Then he turned on his heel and almost before Moorfield had left the room, he was halfway down the stairs again, heading for his mother's boudoir.

'Mamma, she's gone! Fled, without a penny in her purse.' He laughed bitterly. 'Damme, not even a purse! And she's so alone, so vulnerable. She thinks I hate her! I must find her!'

'She can't have gone far,' Lady O'Neill said. She was already dressed, a cloak slung over her shoulders. 'I've ordered the gig, I'm going to drive around the roads and lanes near here. If she's on foot, we should catch up with her fairly quickly.'

'She must be on foot! How else could she travel?'

Even as he said the words, his lordship heard a soft footfall behind him. It was Pamela, wrapped in a silky, flower-embroidered negligée, her hair free from powder, her skin pure and pale in the morning light. It occurred to his lordship that he had never seen her so beautiful, nor had he ever felt more indifferent to her charms.

'How else? Why, with Jerome, of course. She's pretty enough to please a man for a few weeks, and he believes I'm indifferent to him. I suppose he's offered to make her his mistress, and she's accepted. It would be a good thing for a slave to become a kept woman. She'd be fed, clothed, and enjoy a degree of independence. Don't worry about her, Crispin. We've got other things to discuss.'

Lord O'Neill turned and looked into the face he had once considered so beautiful, into the eyes as cool and shallow as the brain behind them.

'You callous, heartless jade,' he said, his voice low. 'You're jealous of her, and no wonder, for she's worth ten of you! God help your husband!' He turned from her to Lady O'Neill. 'I'll get my carriage out and follow them. If Peri did go of her own free will—which I doubt—I'm sure when she hears about her French relatives she'll let me restore her to the place where she belongs. I must go.'

He turned and hurried away down the corridor, leaving Miss Courtney staring after him, her mouth falling open. Lady O'Neill, however, followed him, calling 'Crispin!' And when he turned, brows raised, she added, 'Don't harm Jerome! Please, my dearest, don't harm him. He's not bad, but he has no conception of what she means to you.'

His face was pale and there was ice in his eyes, but a hard grin dawned. 'No violence, eh, Mamma? I promise you that if I find her safe . . .' He swallowed, and the grin wavered for a moment. 'Look, if she's *alive*, if only he's not hurt her ...' he passed a hand over his eyes. 'What I'm trying to say is, if I arrive too late, and she's ... she's ...'

'I know, my son. You want her anyway. I know. Now off with you!'

His lordship gave his mother a glance which blazed with gratitude and then he was gone, dropping down the stairs two at a time, clattering across the hall and out of the house.

Left alone, the two women faced one another. The beauty, seeing the failure of her hopes to win Lord O'Neill as a husband, and his mother, worried for her son and for the child whose fate must now lie in the hands of her libertine nephew.

Miss Courtney was turning away when Lady O'Neill laid a hand on her silk-clad arm.

'My dear child, don't be unhappy. Crispin is my very dear son, but you and he were not suited. You'll find the right man for you, I promise. Peri loved him from the first, and she's no slave, she's a member of the French nobility.'

Slowly, Miss Courtney's face puckered. 'But everyone will say I set my cap at his lordship and couldn't bring him up to the mark,' she wailed. 'And I sent J-J-Jerome awa-ay!'

Lady O'Neill could not help smiling at this ingenuous remark, but she said comfortingly, 'Nonsense, my love! You are so very pretty that everyone will know the truth—that you didn't *want* Crispin, but preferred some other gentleman! I know Mr Wrinstead danced attendance upon you before my son returned home, and there was talk of the Duke of

Drysdale, and Sir Roderick Cowper. And Jerome, of course!'

'Jerome appreciates me,' Miss Courtney agreed, sniffing. 'But if Crispin marries that ... that ...'

'Ah, but if ... I mean when, Crispin brings Peri back here, I shall have to take her straight over to France to meet her relatives. Crispin will come with me, of course. Then, I think, we shall put it about that he met her there for the first time. The servants know Peri, of course, but by a most fortunate chance scarcely anyone else even met her!'

'But I did! I could tell ...'

'Yes, Pamela dear, I know you could. But if you did, I should make sure that everyone knew you had found yourself cast aside for a slave! However, if you say nothing, everyone will assume Crispin married Peri on the rebound after you refused him.'

This thought gave Miss Courtney so much satisfaction that a small smile curled her lips and her eyes, still tear-filled, began to sparkle. Seeing this, Lady O'Neill added with serpentine cunning, 'And regarding Jerome, if you really want to get to know him better, then I'm perfectly willing to speak to your Papa, and assure him that though my nephew was once very wild, it only needs a wife and some responsibility to make him settle down.'

'*Would* you?' breathed Miss Courtney ecstatically.

'Yes, I would. And now dry your eyes and get dressed, and we'll have breakfast together.'

Peri was jerked awake as the coach swung round the corner of what proved to be an inn yard. She peeped out and saw Jerome swing down, shouting to the ostlers to hurry, for he would only get himself a glass of ale and a plate of bread and beef, and then he would expect his coach to be ready for him.

The ostlers, used to changing horses for the mail coaches, nodded and grinned, knowing that whatever Mr Harcourt's faults, he would tip them a guinea if the horses were good ones, and between the shafts before he emerged from the inn.

All too soon for Peri's liking, Jerome strode across the yard, wiping his mouth with the back of his hand, climbed into the coach and called to his groom to set the conveyance in motion.

The coach swung round and Peri poked her head out, intending to slide out of the boot while the coach had still a corner to negotiate and had not picked up speed. But one of the ostlers saw her and shouted, so Peri prudently ducked back into the boot, and by the time the coach was out of sight of the inn it was moving far too fast for her to risk jumping out.

However, Peri was nothing if not game, and she endured the lurching and bumping for another couple of hours, telling herself that discovery or not, she would have to climb out at the next stopping place, or she would be too stiff and bruised to climb out at all.

To her surprise, the next stop was not at a busy inn, but by a stile leading into a leafy wood. She poked her head out, and heard Jerome making a joking remark to his groom about the quantity of ale he had taken aboard at their last stop, and then he disappeared into the wood, leaving the groom up on the seat, with his back to Peri.

Quick as a flash, Peri climbed out of the luggage boot, took one glance at the groom's unconscious back, and then dived into the wood. She would hide until they drove away, and then she would walk to the nearest farm or cottage and ask for employment.

But speed was her undoing. She entered the trees at a crouching run, head down, and found herself caught and held in strong arms.

'What are you ... Good God, it's Peri!' Jerome looked down at her, an expression of astonishment on his face. 'Peri? How came you here?'

'I ran, of course,' Peri said sarcastically. She wriggled. 'Let me *go*, sir!'

But the grip on her shoulders tightened. 'By God, you must have been in the luggage boot! So you're coming to London?'

'I'm leaving Brownlow Hall, anyway,' Peri returned doggedly. She looked frankly up into the dark face above her own. 'Will you take me to London, sir?'

'Of course,' he said softly. 'Of course I will. And perhaps, when we get there ... but time enough to consider that. Have you eaten today?'

She shook her head. 'No. Nor last night.'

His hands slid from her shoulders and he took her wrist in a light clasp. 'Very well, we'll dine earlier than I'd planned.' They returned to the coach and he held open the door for her. 'In with you!'

The groom, turning in time to see his master lifting Peri into the coach, looked extremely startled and

Jerome, taking pity on him, said briefly, 'We had a stowaway, Briggs, in the luggage boot. But she'll travel with me now.'

Briggs, stiffening his face to its former wooden expression, said 'Yes, sir,' and waited until the door was shut before giving a low whistle beneath his breath. So that was the way the land lay!

Inside the coach, Jerome settled into his seat, then leaned across to Peri. 'We'll stop at the Golden Lion for a meal. You must be stiff and you're certainly dirty, coming all that way cramped into the luggage boot. When we get to the inn I'll bespeak a room for you. You didn't bring a change of clothing, I suppose?' Then, as she shook her head, 'Well, while dinner is prepared I suggest you send your gown down to the servants and they'll brush it and iron it for you.'

He let his eyes roam critically over her small person. She was wearing a gown of Selina's which had been altered to fit her. It was a sprigged jaconet, cut low in the bodice, with a flounced skirt and tight-fitting sleeves ending in a froth of lace at the wrists. It was a pretty gown but had got sadly crushed and dirtied in the boot. 'Yes, that would be best. I've no wish to sit down to dinner with you in your present state.'

Peri, glancing down at herself, had to admit there was more than a grain of truth in Jerome Harcourt's strictures but she was tired, and sitting up in the coach the movement which had been so uncomfortable when she was crouching in the boot, became like the rocking of a cradle. Worn out, she soon slept, and

Jerome moved across to sit beside her so that she might lie safely against his shoulder.

Presently he put his arm round her, drawing her close. He looked down at the curve of her dark lashes lying on her pale, tear-stained cheeks. She had fallen into his hands without any effort on his part after all! He let his glance play on the shadow of her cleavage, which he could see as she slumbered against him, and on the rest of her pretty figure. He would wine her, dine her, and bed her, the delicious little creature. And this time there would be no one to interfere. Crispin was miles away, probably making his peace with Pamela.

I mean to do right by the girl, though, he told himself virtuously as the coach ate up the miles. *She shall have a neat apartment in a decent area of town and I'll take her into society, introduce her to my friends, so that when I'm tired of her, someone else can take her over.*

In her sleep she muttered something, moving closer into his casual embrace. He felt an unaccountable tightening of his heartstrings. *If I do tire of her*, he added mentally. And in so doing, realised that for the first time in his life he was proposing to take responsibility for another human being. He wondered uneasily if he would regret seducing Peri. She was so young, and would be totally dependent upon him. Then, glancing down at her again, he was sure he would not. He remembered her dimpling smile, the frank way she spoke, the liveliness of her mind. And he remembered, also, the way it felt to hold her in his arms. He smiled. Whatever else she might do to him, Peri would never bore him!

CHAPTER
TEN

PERI opened her eyes to find that she was being gently shaken, and that the chaise stood still in an inn yard.

'Wake up, Peri! Briggs has bespoken a room for you, and I shall order dinner. Climb down, and an abigail will show you to your room.'

Peri, waking to find herself in Jerome's company, knew a stab of fear, but he looked tired, a trifle impatient, not at all frightening. As she crossed the cobbles beside him, she looked doubtfully up into his face. Would he take the opportunity of being alone with her to start all that hugging and kissing again? But he did not look in the least amorous. He was talking about dinner, asking her which dishes she preferred, and then he handed her over to the abigail and walked towards the coffee-room to interview the landlord without a backward glance, merely saying, 'I'll see you later then, my dear,' before disappearing.

The abigail led her up the stairs and into a pleasant room on the first floor, overlooking the inn yard. The girl said in soft country tones, 'His lordship said you'd want to wash and do your hair. Brushes are in the little case, and soap, and I've brought you hot water and a towel. He said you'd want your gown brushed and ironed too, before you dine.'

'Thank you,' Peri said. 'Can you wait while I slip my gown off? Then you can take it downstairs straight away. You won't keep it for long, will you?'

'No more than ten minutes; the iron's hot,' the girl assured her. And presently she took the gown and went away, leaving Peri, in her petticoat, to the luxury of hot water, soap, and the vigorously plied hairbrush.

Presently a tap on the door indicated that the abigail had been as good as her word. Peri hurried across, unbolted the door—and Jerome strolled into the room and closed the door unhurriedly behind him.

'Everything all right?' he enquired, as if it were the most natural thing in the world to be standing in the bedroom, with Peri in her white petticoat, her hair loose down her back, her skin fresh and tingling from the energetic application of soap and water.

'Yes, everything's all right,' she replied guardedly. 'My gown won't be long.'

He nodded. 'And dinner will be served in an hour, so we've plenty of time to talk.' He took her hand and led her towards the bed. 'Let's sit down and discuss your situation.'

'Not on the bed,' Peri said quickly. 'The abigail will be bringing my gown back in a minute and she might think ... she might say ...'

They were standing beside the bed now and

Jerome sat down on it, reaching out and taking both her hands. He was laughing, devils of amusement dancing in the dark eyes.

'My dear child, your fears are unfounded! The abigail won't be bringing your gown back for the best part of an hour. I met her as she was taking it downstairs and told her I wanted it sponged and pressed properly, and brought back in time for dinner. As to what she'll think, I find I care very little. I've already told the landlord that my wife and I want dinner in an hour.'

She gasped, trying to pull her hands out of his grasp. 'Your *wife*? Sir, he would never believe such a thing! I have no luggage, no change of clothing . . .'

'I don't suppose he believed it for one moment,' Jerome agreed cordially. 'He thinks, of course, that you're my mistress. Well, sweetheart, I intend to prove him right!'

Peri cried out then, as he swung her back on to the pillows without any apparent effort. She struggled, but he was holding her down with his body-weight, her hands only able to hit out feebly at his broad back. He began to kiss her neck, saying as he did so, 'No use crying out. If the abigail hears a cry, she'll doubtless take it for ecstasy! And she'll envy you, for there's more pleasure than pain coming to you, I promise.'

The pillows beneath her were soft and yielding, as was the feather mattress. She moved her head desperately, trying to elude his mouth, but he found her lips, pushing her head deeper into the pillows so that she could not escape, prolonging the kiss.

Peri had never felt more helpless. She was still bruised and stiff from her ride in the luggage boot, and shocked by her own simplicity. She should have known! She made no sound, but the salt tears slid down her face and he tasted them and raised his head.

'What's this? Tears?'

To her immense relief he moved back from her a little, his expression softer than she had ever seen it.

'Look, you don't hate me, do you?'

She did not answer, lying on her back and staring at him whilst the slow tears welled up in her eyes and trickled down her cheeks.

He shook her, but gently. 'Peri! Damn it, what else is there for you?'

Some of her spirit returned at that. She struggled into a sitting position and rubbed the tears from her eyes. 'I could work as an inn servant.'

He laughed. 'And how long do you think it would be before you took some fine gentleman his jug of shaving water and found yourself in his bed? Such a one would take you and cast you aside. You're alone now, Peri, and unprotected. I'm offering to be your protector.'

She swayed, putting a hand to her head. 'Oh, how strange I feel! As if . . .'

Jerome seemed to lean over sideways, and then the floor came rushing dizzyingly up at her. She felt herself sliding helplessly, felt something cold strike her cheek, and then she was gone from there, into darkness.

She came round to find herself sitting on the edge

of the bed, with her head pressed down on to her knees and a hand resting on the back of her neck. She stirred, whimpering, and heard Jerome say reassuringly, 'It's all right, Peri, you fainted. Fool that I am, trying to seduce you when you've not eaten all day, and had ridden in that wretched boot! Your gown is ready, so we can go and dine now.'

'And what shall we do afterwards?' Peri said suspiciously, walking carefully over to the door, and was annoyed when he laughed.

'Let afterwards take care of itself.'

They had an excellent meal and Peri, almost forgetting her troubles, made up for her long fast, though she would not touch the wine which Jerome tried to press upon her. She ate her dessert as slowly as possible, and toyed with the cheese, but the inevitable moment came at last.

'Off we go,' Jerome said cheerfully, taking her by the elbow and leading her to the foot of the stairs. In a lower tone he added, 'Don't be afraid I'll pounce on you the moment the door closes. We'll discuss this thing sensibly, I promise you.'

Peri, remembering the sharp steak-knife which she had hidden in the sleeve of her gown during dinner, trotted upstairs ahead of her would-be protector quite cheerfully. She had decided what she must do. She would enter the room first, then turn and present the knife to Jerome's ribs. Having driven him out of the bedroom, she sincerely hoped that a good night's rest would bring its own council, for at the moment, her mind had only room for one thought; that she would not become Jerome's mistress until she was quite certain there was no alternative.

But Jerome was no fool. He followed close on her heels so that they arrived in the bedroom together and she had not even managed to get hold of the knife.

'And now I'll take that knife,' he said pleasantly, holding out his hand. 'What a vixen you are! Would you really have stabbed me with it?'

Wearily, Peri fumbled in her sleeve for the knife, but was given no opportunity of turning it on her tormentor. He coolly took it from her and pocketed it, then sat down on the bed and patted the place beside him.

Peri noticed that he had not locked the door, but was careful not to let her eyes stray in that direction. Was there just a chance that she might escape from him even yet?

'Come and sit down, and we'll talk,' Jerome said.

This time, however, Peri intended to make her feelings plain from the start. 'No!' she retorted, glaring at him. 'No, and no, and no! I shall fight, and bite, and scratch. I shall not come near you!'

He grinned, a gleam lighting the devils in his eyes once more. 'Indeed? Well, perhaps even a fighting Peri would be preferable to a tearful, fainting one. I enjoy fighting pretty women!'

'I shall make tears also,' Peri said gamely. 'And, perhaps, faint!'

He laughed and got to his feet, coming across towards her. He had slipped his coat off and the white frilled shirt made him look enormous. As he advanced towards her, he quite deliberately began to unfasten his shirt. She could see the breadth of his chest, the dark hair curling across it, and when he took a deep breath she saw his rib-cage lift and spread.

She found this slow, deliberate advance really terrifying, but dared not show it. She backed further into the corner, the wild beating of her heart almost suffocating her, and prepared to defend herself.

When he was within a foot of her she kicked out at his shins with all her force and then, in wild terror, clawed at his throat.

He laughed on a low note, caught the neck of her gown, and ripped it almost down to the waist. Startled, she clutched the garment, trying to cover herself, and was helpless to prevent him gathering her up in his arms and carrying her over to the bed. He dumped her on it without ceremony, and caught at her gown again, ripping it further to reveal her small, pointed breasts. He knelt over her, lust gleaming in his eyes, flaring his nostrils, voluptuously curving his mouth. He looked the embodiment of evil to the terrified girl beneath him.

'No! No!' Peri cried, and kicked out, realising her mistake even as he caught her ankles in a cruel grip, and wrenched her skirt and petticoat up, nearly smothering her in the layers of material. She fought free to see his face poised above her, his body lowering itself on to her.

Then there was a crash, an oath, and he had gone! She sat up, clutching the torn gown, then got shakily off the bed.

Lord O'Neill stood there, white fury blazing on his face. Jerome, his shirt unbuttoned, his dark hair in wild disarray, stood facing him, breathing heavily, an ugly look replacing the heavy lust which had so terrified Peri.

'Get out of here, damn you!'

That was Lord O'Neill, and Peri saw his knuckles whiten round the stock of the whip he carried.

Jerome said, quite slowly and pleasantly, 'This is my room. I've hired it for myself and my whore. Now *you* get out!'

Lord O'Neill moved so quickly that Peri scarcely saw him except as a blur. Jerome could not have had time to lift a finger to defend himself before he was stretched out, senseless, on the floor. His lordship's fist had caught him right on the point of his jaw and had lifted him off his feet with the strength of it.

Peri, with a delighted gasp, caught Jerome's shoulders and began to drag him towards the door.

'Let's throw him downstairs, sir,' she urged, glancing up at her deliverer. 'I meant to lock him out, or kill him with a knife, but he was too clever for me.'

'Are you all right?' His lordship, breathing hard, helped her to bundle Jerome's inanimate form out of the room, then he glanced at her torn gown and dishevelled hair and quickly looked away. 'Here, wrap this round you.' He tore the bedspread off the bed and handed it to her.

'I'll lock the door,' Peri said, suiting action to words. 'Yes, I'm all right. Have you ... have you come to rescue me? But how? You cannot take me back to the Hall. Miss Courtney would never allow it.'

'Damn Miss Courtney,' his lordship said roundly. 'She's nothing to me. Our betrothal is broken off, isn't it? Yes, I've come to take you home, back to the Hall, where you belong.'

'Not to my French relatives? Oh, good!'

He had been standing a foot away from her, devouring her with his eyes, but now he said incredulously, 'You know! But how? Was it Jerome? By God, if he knew, and still took you away and tried to seduce you, I'll kill him even if I hang for it.'

'I listened,' Peri answered promptly. 'I was in the dressing-room and I heard. That was why I ran away. I hid in Jerome's luggage boot, but he found me.'

'You heard! Then you must know that I wanted to marry you, that Mamma and I planned to take you back to France after you and I had become betrothed ... Did you not want me, then?'

'Not want you? Oh, my dear lord, I knew nothing of that! I ran away when you said I was a ... a scheming wretch, and that you would *not* marry me!'

He went to her then, like a magnet to a pin, and gathered her into his arms, kissing the face turned up to his, muttering against the smooth skin, 'I love you, Peri! I want to marry you more than anything else in the world.'

'You would not rather just make me your mistress?' She moved back a little, her eyes wide on his face, one finger tracing the line of his lips. 'Do you know, Jerome did not just want to seduce me, he wanted to make me his mistress!'

Lord O'Neill took her by the shoulders, an incredulous expression stealing into his blue eyes. 'Peri. What means seduce?'

She laughed at his use of her favourite phrase, but said, 'Why, to kiss and cuddle! I know *that*! But to be a man's mistress, Milord, is much more! Why, he tore my gown off, he ...'

Lord O'Neill shook his head. 'Don't tell me. I promised Mamma that I'd not hurt him.' He shivered, his blue eyes moving hotly across the small, tear-stained face, the swollen mouth, down to where bruises were already showing on her shoulders and breasts where Jerome's hard fingers had gripped her. 'He didn't ... hurt you, my little love?'

She leaned against him, putting her arms round his neck, letting the bedspread fall, unheeded, to the floor. 'Of course not! You came! So shall I be your mistress?'

He was trembling and the colour, which had drained from his face as he entered the bedroom, was stealing back. He said hoarsely, 'No, Peri. I want to marry you! I love you, damn it!'

'And I love you, your darling lordship!'

She stood on tiptoe to kiss him but he put her back from him, slipping off his coat, and held it out to her.

'Put that on, and I'll go downstairs and get my bag from the curricle. Mamma did not know that I should find you in ... in such a case, but she realised you'd not got clothing or toiletries with you. She packed a gown and a pelisse and some other feminine fripperies. You can put them on, and then we'll drive home.'

Peri opened her mouth to protest and was interrupted by a voice from the other side of the door.

'Crispin? You pack quite a punch, my buck! I take it that you aren't going to marry Pamela after all?'

Lord O'Neill turned round and said coldly to his unseen cousin, 'That's right.'

'Then you may have my room and welcome. I shall drive straight back to Brownlow Hall and try my luck with the lady.'

'You'd best be gone before we arrive home,' his lordship said uncompromisingly. The voice outside the door changed to a more persuasive note.

'Don't be like that, old fellow! How was I to know you loved the chit? Look, if you stay at this place tonight, you'll not get home much before dinner time tomorrow. That will give me plenty of time to talk Pamela round, and to whisk her off to London to visit her Papa!'

'Go to hell,' advised his lordship briefly. Peri was standing so close to him that the scent of her filled his nostrils, and she had let his coat remain open so that he dared not look down for fear his resolution to behave like a gentleman might dissolve.

'Oh come on, Crispin, think of me! You've got what you want, why shouldn't I have what I want?'

Peri twinkled at his lordship. 'Why not indeed?'

she murmured, casting his coat down in a very ungrateful manner and putting her arms round his neck. 'Who would ever know, sir?'

'I mean, who need ever know that you were her first choice?' echoed the voice through the door panelling. 'All I'm asking is that you remain here for one night!'

'That's all I'm asking,' Peri said. His lordship looked down at her. She was wearing her most beguiling expression and very little else, his lordship realised, his resolution wavering.

'Oh come on, Cris, give me a chance,' Jerome implored.

His lordship bent his head and his lips met Peri's. Softly, softly, he parted her lips, telling himself that to kiss her was no sin. Against his shirt front, he could feel the warmth and shape of her breasts as he crushed her close.

'Cris! I say, Crispin! Answer me, damn you!'

Peri seemed to be melting against him, and gentleness was forgotten. His mouth crushed hers every bit as forcefully as Jerome's had, but she only strained him closer, giving a little murmur of pure pleasure.

'Very well, I'll return to Brownlow Hall with or without your consent!'

Outside the door, Jerome cocked his head, waiting for a response.

Nothing. Silence. He raised his fist to bang on the door, to insist that his cousin listen to him—and stopped, hand in mid-air.

He listened a moment longer, then a slow smile

curved his mouth and without another word, he turned and went slowly downstairs.

And his lordship, giving way at long last to his baser instincts, held a slender, silk-skinned Peri tightly to his thumping heart, and murmured against her hair, 'Oh, my darling! My darling Rachelle Blanche Nicolette Perigand!'

Masquerade
Historical Romances

Intrigue excitement romance

Masquerade
Historical Romances

Intrigue
excitement
romance

DAUGHTER OF ISIS
by Belinda Grey

A few weeks ago she had been Ellen Parry of Cwm Bedd
in Wales, never likely to travel very much further afield.
Now she was in the land of the pyramids, and a mysterious
man on a white horse seemed determined to block her
every move . . .

STRANGER IN THE GLEN
by Isobel Stewart

When her parents died, Rosemary Lockhart made her
home with her mother's old friend, Elspeth Macrae of
Glen Ardrachan. But when Elspeth's Jacobite son
returned home, he made it clear that *he* had no welcome
for a stranger — particularly an English girl!

Look out for these titles in your local paperback shop from
12th June 1981

Mills & Boon
Best Seller Romances

The very best of Mills & Boon Romances
brought back for those of you who missed
them when they were first published.

In May
we bring back the following four
great romantic titles.

COUNTRY OF THE FALCON
by Anne Mather

When Alexandra went to the uncivilised regions of the Amazon
to look for her father she was prepared to find life different
from the security of her English home. She certainly didn't
expect, however, to find herself at the mercy of the devastatingly
attractive Declan O'Rourke and to be forced to accompany him
to his mountain retreat at Paradiablo.

FORBIDDEN RAPTURE
by Violet Winspear

When Della Neve went on a Mediterranean cruise, she wasn't
looking for a holiday romance. Her future was already bound to
Marsh Graham, the fiancé to whom she owed everything. But on
board ship she encountered Nicholas di Fioro Franquila, who
treated women as playthings. Was Della an exception?

THE BENEDICT MAN
by Mary Wibberley

Lovely surroundings and a kind and considerate employer —
Beth was delighted at the prospect of her new job in Derbyshire.
But when she arrived at Benedict House she discovered that it
was not the sympathetic Mrs. Thornburn who required her
services as a secretary, but her arrogant and completely unreason-
able nephew. Could Beth put up with his insufferable attitude
towards her?

TILL THE END OF TIME
by Lilian Peake

As far as Marisa was concerned Dirk was no longer part of her
life. So it came as a great shock to her when he returned, even
more dictatorial and exasperating than she remembered him,
to disrupt her calm again. Of course, it wasn't as if he meant
anything to her now. Yet why did she find herself wondering
about his relationship with the glamorous Luella?

If you have difficulty in obtaining any of these books through
your local paperback retailer, write to:

Mills & Boon Reader Service
P.O. Box 236, Thornton Road, Croydon, Surrey, CR9 3RU.